I0527466

BY DON SWAIM

Man with Two Faces
The Assassination of Ambrose Bierce: A Love Story
Steampunk Electroblaster Romance
Bright Sun Extinguished: Ode to Norman Mailer
The H.L. Mencken Murder Case

DON SWAIM
MAN WITH TWO FACES

DON SWAIM
MAN WITH TWO FACES

MONTAG

First Montag Press E-Book and Paperback Original Edition April 2018

Montag Press
ISBN: 978-1-940233-54-3
Design © 2018 Rick Febré
Vector files by Vecteezy
Author photo © 2018 Elizabeth Joyce

Montag Press Team:
Project Editor – Charlie Franco
Managing Director – Charlie Franco

A Montag Press Book
www.montagpress.com
Montag Press
1066 47th Ave. Unit #9
Oakland CA 94601 USA

Printed & Digitally Originated in the United States of America
10 9 8 7 6 5 4 3 2 1

*It's almost worth the Great Depression to learn
how little our big men know.*
Will Rogers

I ask you to judge me by the enemies I have made.
Franklin D. Roosevelt

*Wherever men are fightin' for their rights,
That's where I'm a-gonna be, Ma.
That's where I'm a-gonna be.*
Woody Guthrie

FEDERAL BUREAU OF INVESTIGATION

MEMORANDUM

To: J. EDGAR HOOVER, Director
From: MIKE LITVAK, Special Agent
Date: December 7, 1941

Re: Tokoloshe and Son Cleansing Services

First, I would like to extend my appreciation for
reinstating me as a special agent. I was most unhappy
in my interim job as a security guard at Wanamaker's
Department Store in Philadelphia, and am glad to be
back in the agency's good graces. For my inadvertent
leaking of classified FBI information to Walter Winchell
I apologize. I had no idea he would actually use the
material on the air.

Understandably, some portions of this memo may need
to be redacted because of the sensitive nature of the
particulars.

Per your request, I have put together this fact sheet
so that some light may shine on the enigmatic Mr.
Tokol Tokoloshe as well as his companion Miss Diana
Dryad, both of whom have vanished under mysterious

circumstances. Tokoloshe was useful to the FBI on more than one occasion as an independent contractor, which included assisting in exposing a Nazi spy ring and capturing Public Enemy Number One, although he displayed too much of an independent attitude to be an actual agent.

Despite my own personal acquaintance with Tokoloshe, there is much we do not know about him, and probably never will. However, the hearsay that he was an alien sent to this planet from another world is false.

We have no knowledge of his birthplace. Because of his familiarity with the Midwest it is assumed he may have been born there, perhaps in Iowa, although he claimed to be fluent in a number of languages, including German, French, Arabic, Mandarin, and Hindi. He referred to an uncle who took him as a child on excursions to McComb, Mississippi, and Enid, Oklahoma, but we have not been able to determine the name or whereabouts of this reputed uncle.

Tokoloshe's real name is unknown. He adopted the pseudonym after a falling out in either Detroit or Cleveland with a man known only as Janus, who swore vengeance on Tokoloshe following the death of a man with whom they were both infatuated. Tokoloshe's assumed name appears to spring from either ancient Arabic or Chinese folklore in which a clever gnome is able to alter his colors like a chameleon, thus fooling his enemies. In that vein, Tokoloshe learned to apply various disguises to hide his identity.

In the relevant time period, 1934-1940, Tokoloshe
appeared to be in his mid to late thirties, suggesting that
his birth date was around 1900.

He did not serve in the War to End All Wars, although
he was an enlistee in the French Foreign Legion in
Morocco. It was probably there that he became enamored
of guns and other armaments. He was also embroiled
in the conflict in the Holy Land, where he became
intimately involved with the late Lawrence of Arabia. It
is speculated that the two men had an affair of a sexual
nature.

How Tokoloshe acquired his wealth has not been fully
established. He made casual reference to diamond
dealing, but rumors that he was involved in the heist
of the massive Lavender Star of Africa have been
thoroughly discredited. It is known, however, that he was
once a rum runner out of Havana, which was the likely
source of his fortune.

Despite claiming that he had little need for funds, he
opened Tokoloshe and Son Cleansing Services in
Manhattan in which he accepted certain dangerous
and secret assignments on behalf of questionable
causes. Our agents have assiduously attempted to
unearth Tokoloshe's business partner and son, but
the younger man has remained elusive. Tokoloshe
engaged a telephone answering service operated by Mrs.
Prunella Mayhem, although she emphatically denies any
connection and hangs up the phone when we try to speak
to her.

He maintained an account with Banque Cantonale de Genève in Switzerland, but it is impossible to determine the amount of his assets or whether the account still exists. The locations and amounts of any other of his assets are uncertain.

While not Sicilian, Tokoloshe was once a soldier in the Castrogiovanni Crime Family, although one of low rank. Confidential informants suggest he was involved in the Mafia's Castellammarese War in 1930 in which the notorious La Cosa Nostra figure Gaetano Gagliano saved Tokoloshe's life, for which he was ever grateful. Gagliano, who became his personal gun dealer, currently operates a convenience store in The Bronx.

Tokoloshe may also have helped to spark a Chinese tong war in a bid to control the distribution of opium, and briefly served as a bodyguard to Senator Huey Long, who was later assassinated. Most recently, we have indications that he was sent to Casablanca to spy on Nazis for a federal intelligence agency, but we lack hard evidence.

While he wore conservative apparel from Hart Schaffner & Marx, as well as safari attire from Best and Company, Tokoloshe usually shopped at the five-and-dime. He rented a well-appointed office suite in the Woolworth Building, yet he considered himself an ascetic and stayed most nights in a tenement room on The Bowery. However, he was impeccable about his clothes, which were cleaned at a Chinese hand-laundry on Hester Street.

It is thought that he kidnapped Aimee Semple
McPherson, the celebrated California revivalist and
sexual bon vivant, after their torrid love affair went
awry. She was released when a ransom was paid.

Tokoloshe and Diana Dryad first became acquainted
in Budapest, although what the two were doing in
Hungary is to be determined. Dryad is the name for a
tree nymph in Hebrew mythology, but whether that was
her given name has not been established. While her past
is murky, we have determined she was raised in East
Asia to parents who were big game hunters or, possibly,
Bible salespeople. In any event, she became sufficiently
proficient with a blowgun to be considered dangerous.
Her pet python Kevin kept her supplied with venom for
her darts.

While she and her parents were impoverished, Dryad
came to be wealthy as the creator of several of radio's
most successful afternoon soap operas. She was a close
acquaintance of broadcast moguls Paley and Sarnoff, and
served as Miss Television at the 1939 World's Fair.

Aviation records indicate that Dryad became a licensed
pilot in 1937. Subsequently, she crashed her plane in
Saskatchewan, Canada, but recovered after suffering
serious injuries. She owned a penthouse apartment at
Park Avenue and Seventy-Fourth Street, where she also
operated her radio scripting business. That apartment is
currently up for sale.

It was primarily through Dryad's radio empire that Tokoloshe, enamored by athletics, became acquainted with an immense variety of professional sports figures, such as George Herman Ruth, Jr., Jim Thorpe, Jesse Owens, Bobby Jones, and Don Budge. Because of their shared interest in sports, Tokoloshe had a relationship with Walter Winchell, and while Tokoloshe made known his dislike for the columnist, Winchell was useful in funneling to him certain information, which was reciprocated.

I hesitate to reveal, sir, that Tokoloshe frequently expressed his distaste toward you, describing you as an officious, tyrannical, cross-dressing despot, certainly a misapprehension on his part, as you have never been known to be officious or tyrannical. In fact, sir, it would not be an understatement to say you are adored outside of the Bureau.

Tokoloshe's preferred mode of travel was rail, but when speed was important would take commercial flights or the de Havilland DH.82 Tiger Moth owned by Dryad. The two were once passengers on the Hindenburg, but apparently not on the date of its fatal explosion. Normally, in traveling overseas, Tokoloshe would sail on the Queen Mary or the Rex, and sometimes tramp steamers. He owned several automobiles, which he stored in strategic locations, and often employed a chauffeur.

Although a teetotaler, he habitually smoked a hookah. He admitted he was once addicted to opium, but kicked

the habit aside from occasional relapses. In Ethiopia,
Tokoloshe learned to play the didgeridoo, a traditional
African wind instrument, and while it is well established
that he despised jazz, he once performed with Glenn
Miller's orchestra.

I hope these facts provide a better understanding of Mr.
Tokoloshe, and you can be assured of their accuracy.
Although his whereabouts and those of Miss Dryad are
currently unknown, please note that our special task
force will remain on the case and eternally vigilant as
long as you are in office.

Respectfully,

M. Litvak

Mike Litvak, Special Agent

one

Man With Two Faces 1934

The Man With Two Faces had returned to New York.

To kill me.

Manhattan glowed with skyscrapers and light, marble-floored hotels trimmed with bronze, museums filled with statuary and Old Masters, foie gras and lobster overflowing at the priciest restaurants, while in Central Park the remnants of Hooverville and its jerry-rigged shacks of the unemployed were still being demolished to make way for the new Great Lawn.

Janus disembarked from the S.S. *Rex* at Pier 86 after a first-class voyage on which the soprano Rosa Ponselle sang Schubert's "Nacht und Träume" in a ship-to-shore radio transmission heard round the world.

In truth, I had half been expecting him. Maybe it was inevitable. Or perhaps my conscience was rattling. Confirmation of his arrival came directly from Walter Winchell at Table 50 in the Cub Room of the Stork Club on East 53rd.

"I'm bushed, Tokol," the *Daily Mirror* columnist and Blue Network commentator told me over White Russians: one part Kahlúa, one part vodka, one part heavy cream. "I'm not getting enough sleep."

"Edison only needed four hours a night, Walter," I said.

"Edison never had a daily column to write."

Winchell, who never revealed his sources, was a prick,

but he was my prick. Whenever I had the goods, I fed him dirt for his gossip pile, and he'd return the favor.

Not known for whispering, he leaned in close and whispered into my ear, "I gotta flash for you. Watch your ass. Janus is in New York looking for you."

After thanking Winchell I slipped him a Benjamin. Bastard always took it, and he was flush.

The Depression hurt. The newspapers told us so. But now, at least, we could drown our troubles in untamed abandon thanks to the repeal of the Eighteenth Amendment. Unless you sold apples or pencils on the street or lived in the Dust Bowl, it was the age of romance: Garbo, Dietrich, Harlow, Lombard—Busby Berkeley.

The era was all about speed. Only the breadlines were slow.

It was easy to tell the bad guys. They wielded tommy guns like John Dillinger, cut down on the bloody Chicago streets by the feds, or they ostentatiously flashed monogrammed gold cigarette cases, lighters, tie clasps, and cufflinks—as did The Man With Two Faces.

It was purely coincidental that *The Man With Two Faces*, the Edward G. Robinson-Mary Astor flick, was unreeling at the Strand in Times Square. Not impressed, I sat through the matinee. Better were the Donald Duck short, Pete Smith Specialty, and the Metrotone newsreel showing Hitler and Mussolini mutually heel-clicking in Italy.

Janus and I went way back. We first met while in the Legion, both enlistees in Morocco south of Fez fighting Berber tribesmen in the Rif mountains. More than drinking pals, we shared our Midwestern American pasts, I from Kansas he from Nebraska. As a young man he was enamored by the impalement arts and wanted to be a professional knife thrower in a carnival. He always carried with him an exquisite set of throwing knives he would use to perform awesome and dangerous feats.

"Eighteen feet," he would tell me. "Always stand eighteen-feet from your target."

But later, in some waterfront dive in Singapore, we had a boozy falling out. Not over the six-thousand carat Lavender Star of Africa, largest diamond known to exist, which made us both impossibly rich, but over a woman. Isn't it always?

I'll always remember Singapore as the place where The Man With Two Faces and I parted ways.

Because of my share of the gem, I never needed to work again. Still, my needs were crudely simple.

I slept at the Y. Frequently, however, I crashed at the penthouse of Diana Dryad, my fiancée and creator and writer of record of radio's most popular network serials, but at night was the nymph of the urban tower, mountain forest, and green valley. No one could fire a blunderbuss, parry with a vorpal sword, or wield a bow and arrow with as much accuracy as she. And what she could do with her blowgun was astonishing.

She had spent her childhood in the Amazon rainforests of Ecuador where her parents were missionaries.

Believing it was a form of onanistic indulgence not to be without gainful labor, I opened shop in a panoramic suite on the sixty-third floor of the Chrysler Building. Mine was highly particularized work in which I performed special, often risky services for a select clientele, which sometimes took me around the world.

I named my business Tokoloshe and Son Cleansing Services. There was no son, of course. That was a diversion, and while I *was* a cleaner of sorts, it was never with a broom or mop.

My name, Tokoloshe, sprang from Zulu mythology, about which I learned during my years in the sub-Sahara: an impish sprite employed to engage in certain behaviors toward others that might be considered malevolent. Legend had it that merely by drinking water the Tokoloshe became invisible—not that I was a sprite, nor did I often drink water.

Thus, I was known as Tokol—or Tokee to my fiancée—which was no more my real name than Janus, The Man With Two Faces, was the actual name of my adversary.

On behalf of my clients I actualized, in strictest confidence, certain results. Such services came at a high price, not because I needed capital, but because my work was uncommonly dangerous. And I put a high price on danger. Usually, I would accept only one or two assignments a year.

Such as a delicate project aimed at forever silencing Huey Long, Louisiana's share-the-wealth populist, known to be preparing a bid for the White House. After he consorted with radio fascist Father Charles Coughlin, it became clear what the unscrupulous Kingfish's destiny had to be, the resolution of which would come in due time.

Many of my days were spent giving away my fortune. Anonymously. It was assumed Roosevelt's Works Progress Administration, the WPA, was financed solely by American tax dollars, but my role in its expansion was, as I intended, never publicly acknowledged.

After Winchell alerted me to the pending threat from my potential assassin, I gazed from my office window at the myriad lights of Manhattan while plotting a course of action. I had three options: waiting for Janus to find me, locating him first, or disappearing.

I was not inclined to disappear.

Janus was not a private man. When in town, he quartered

at the Waldorf Towers, frequented the chorus-girl spectacle between movies at the Hippodrome, first-nighted the Broadway shows, and attended every bout at the Garden. He was wild about prizefighting.

Despite our once close relationship, we were not alike.

While he tooled about in a Daimler driven by a white-gloved chauffeur, I was a straphanger on the Third Avenue El, and never kept any car I bought. He dined at Passy, I the Automat. Bonwit's was his preferred shopping mecca, mine Kresge's. He hobnobbed with celebrities such as Rudy Vallee, Clark Gable, Ted Lewis, and Errol Flynn. I, mostly, reveled in my anonymity—usually disguising myself in a mustache when on the town—although I counted Diego Rivera, Sinclair Lewis, and Ira Gershwin among my cronies, not the least being Groucho Marx. Not being a fan of professional sports, I never had an interest in hobnobbing with athletes, other than an occasional boxer.

I was content mingling with the merchant seamen on the East River docks, the fishmongers on Fulton Street, the Mohawk iron workers erecting the city's skyscrapers, and the girls at Polly Adler's whorehouse, the Majestic, on West 75th. Whenever I ran short of cash—I traveled light—Ira was always good for a ten spot. Groucho, on the other hand, was tight with a buck.

Then it came to me like a gloved fist to the jaw.

When I read in Hearst's *American* that Max Baer was about to take on Primo Carnera for the world heavyweight championship, I was certain The Man With Two Faces would be at ringside. Because the Garden only accommodated twenty-thousand spectators, the promoters decided to move the fight to the outdoor Madison Square Garden Bowl in Long Island City, which entertained seventy-two thousand. There I could perform my deed and fade casually into the crowd.

Diego Rivera and I met frequently in the tiny Qué Chingados Chili House—four tables—on Bleecker Street in Greenwich Village, where, only if accepted by the Cojoines family, the proprietors, one could eat authentic Mexican cuisine, which otherwise was unheard of in pastrami-centric New York.

"I worry about you, Tokol, *mi amigo*. If you do this thing…"

So said Diego after I revealed to him my lethal scheme.

Except for Ira Gershwin, I was as close to Diego as any man I knew, although his English was as shaky as my Spanish. He was still smarting after being shafted by the Rockefellers, who chiseled Rivera's "Man at the Crossroads" mural out of the wall in the lobby of the new Radio City skyscraper. Why? It included images of Vladimir Lenin and a May Day parade.

"It's a matter of survival, Diego. He'll kill me unless I act first."

"The police…"

"That's a laugh. Neither Janus nor I can go to the police. Ever."

"You both did something—how you say?—nefarious?"

"An understatement."

Despite our mutual affinity, I still couldn't tell Rivera that Janus and I, when we were in Africa, pulled off the biggest diamond heist in history, abetted by a dazzling jungle princess for whom we both had an unholy attachment—which, through a series of unplanned and egregious acts, led to our rupture.

And her death.

It occurred while The Man With Two Faces was performing his death-defying knife-throwing performance, intending to create a silhouette of knives around our African beauty. He had never missed before, and it's clear I drunkenly caused his distraction. For which he never forgave me.

I experienced unfathomable remorse—yet our obscene wealth, mine and The Man With Two Faces, had been left intact. If it could only have been the other way…

Although Janus knew me too well, perhaps better than I knew myself, I was reasonably certain he would never find me in New York, despite his unlimited resources. While I had covered my tracks suitably—or so I thought—I had a vulnerability.

That time in Macau in the Pearl River Delta Hotel and Grill when I let down my defenses, and, in the liquid intimacy of our suite, he and I… I'll say no more, except to admit I revealed, body and soul, too much of myself.

And now he wanted me dead.

How many Automats would his henchmen have to stake out before they came upon me inserting a dime in the slot for a slice of apple cobbler? The blueberry pie wasn't bad either.

Diego Rivera, of course, had his own problems, notably his marriage to the tempestuous artist Frida Kahlo. That Frida had had an affair with Leon Trotsky didn't help. Expelled from the Communist Party while at the same time menaced by fascists and their apologists, the besieged Rivera was rarely without his pistol.

Little wonder we were chums.

It was widely speculated that the Rockefellers, despite cravenly destroying Diego's mural, paid him his $21,000 commission anyway. Untrue. It was I who secretly financed Rivera's commission, and then reimbursed the Rockefellers another $50,000 to keep their mouths shut. Greedy bastards. Naturally, I never told Diego. He was a man who put a high price on self-respect.

So I waited for my inevitable confrontation with The Man With Two Faces.

At the Seaglades nightclub in the St. Regis Hotel, Vincent Lopez and his Orchestra performed "Nola," broadcasting their regular live remote on WJZ. There, she sipping mai tais, I gin rickies, I told Diana Dryad everything. Until then she had not known about The Man With Two Faces.

Dressed in slithery satin and wearing a broach of marcasite and onyx, Diana dragged on a Viceroy, her preferred brand, through her six-inch bakelite holder.

"Why didn't you tell me about this before, Tokee, darling? I thought we pledged always to be honest with one another."

"A sin of omission not dishonesty, dollface. First, I didn't want to worry you, and second, I thought it would never come to this."

"You were wrong on both counts."

"I was naïve to say the least."

"What are you going to do about it?"

"Eliminate him."

"That simple, darling? Really?"

"Unless he gets to me first. I've no intention of allowing Janus to come between you and me." I paused, nearly choked up. "To be candid, I've been through this before."

"What are you saying?"

"Prior to my entering your world, I lost someone dear to me, and while both I and The Man With Two Faces share the responsibility for what led to her death, he blames me."

"And *are* you to blame, darling?"

"I, I... It's complicated."

The music stopped, and we heard the tuxedo-attired announcer, whose voice I knew to be that of André Baruch—or was it Pierre Andrei? I sometimes got them confused—enunciate into the microphone.

"We interrupt this broadcast for the latest news on Amelia Earhart, whose plane has just landed at Roosevelt Field, Long Island. It was her second solo flight across the Atlantic, this time from Brussels to New York in fourteen-hours, fifty-three minutes, surpassing her own record, in a specially-equipped Lockheed Vega supplied with extra fuel tanks."

The entire Seaglades burst into applause as Vincent Lopez again picked up his baton.

Diana and I were no strangers to flight. Only the previous year we were among the passengers aboard the *Graf Zeppelin* in a trans-Atlantic junket to London. But the accommodations were not up to her standards—it had no heating and the German food was nauseating—so we returned to America on the *Queen Mary*.

I explained to skeptical Diana my plans to dispatch The Man With Two Faces at the coming Baer-Carnera bout.

"Too many people on the premises for your purposes, I fear," she said.

"On the contrary. They'll be my camouflage."

"Hmmm."

She squeezed my hand.

Tipsy, Diana and I hailed a Checker to haul us to her Park Avenue penthouse, where, shedding our clothes, we waltzed naked into the bedroom with the four poster. There we performed our magic, she as a nymph, I as a sprite.

Her lavish apartment was filled with palisander wood cabinets and marble tops, gold-leaf mirrors, clocks of ivory and enamel, hammered metal vases inlaid with copper and silver, glass figurines in fast motion, sculptures of silver and coral, ferro-nickel dishware, bronzed statuary of women in flight, terra-cotta nymphs in majestic poses, wrought-iron bookends of leaping gazelles, framed engravings by Rockwell Kent, bon-bon boxes with stenciled designs and silvered filigree, Chinese fans with geometric mother-of-pearl patterns, aluminum and Lucite floor lamps.

Commanding her bedroom was an oversized archery target on which she, from her bed, practiced with her blow-gun and, occasionally, her crossbow. Let me not forget her pet king cobra Kyle. I treated him gingerly because he was eighteen-feet long with a bad disposition and had the run of the suite. I was certain Kyle would turn on me once Diana's back was turned.

Sometimes it all made me dizzy, and I needed to return to my spartan, narrow bed at the Y on West 63rd.

During the day, Diana's penthouse was turned into a ra-dio factory, where she directed a bevy of writers pecking at Underwoods as they composed, under her name, most of the day-time serials on the Red, Blue, and Columbia networks. "Our Gal Zelda," "Frank Hummert's Wife," "Elaine's Marriage," "When a Widow Weds," and too many others to list. She had the webs in the palm of her hand, and the sponsors locked up: Pillsbury, Procter & Gamble, Post Cereals, General Foods.

Diana's radio world had conspired with the talkies to kill off vaudeville, and sometimes I missed those grand old come-dy teams: Ticknor & Fields, Doubleday & Doran, Harcourt & Brace, Simon & Schuster, and Little & Brown.

As time passed, I remained cautious.

Waiting for that inevitable Thursday night in Queens when I would erase from my life The Man With Two Faces.

One evening, after applauding an experimental play by an unknown playwright named Clifford Odets at the Stage Left Theater on the Lower East Side, Rivera and I made our way to McSorley's for a brew or three. On Delancey Street, I got the uneasy feeling we were being followed, although when I discreetly turned I saw no one suspicious, which of course raised my suspicions. My instincts were seldom wrong.

Was it possible that Janus had tracked me?

"What's the matter, *mi amigo?*" Diego said. "You seem distracted. Is someone behind us?"

"It may be nothing, but—"

"Do not worry. I've got my pistol. Probably just some *matón*—how you say?—goon from the Rockefellers wanting to torment me."

"Whoever it may be, it's best we split up, Diego. You go south on Essex Street and fade into Chinatown. I'll head north. You shouldn't be seen with me for awhile. It's not safe."

Rivera nodded. "I understand and do as you say." He put his hand on my shoulder. "*Buena suerte, mi amigo.*"

Clearly, it wasn't prudent to return either to my room at the Y or to Diana's penthouse. Instead, I swiped the ratty old coat of a snoring wino sprawled on the sidewalk, while gently draping my own camel-hair overcoat over him. I actually knew the poor bastard. He had the misfortune of being a broker in a Wall Street bucket shop on Black Tuesday. Wearing the alky's coat and blending in with the bums on The Bowery, I settled for the night on a cot in a fifty-cent cage in a flophouse. It was a decent enough sleep, despite the coughs and shrieks and stench. I'd experienced worse in Africa.

The following morning, I lined up for the free coffee and doughnuts, and in return listened politely to women in rimless glasses and middle-parted hair explaining the blessings of Christ, the renunciation of sin, and the joys of the everlasting. The coffee was almost worth it, but the doughnuts were stale.

Determined to shake off the possibility of a tail, circuitously I worked my way up to Canal Street where I took the

Lexington line to Grand Central, closest stop to the New York Public Library. Coalescing among the scurrying commuters in the terminal, and after eating clams at the Oyster Bar, I hiked to the library's main reading room to examine books on the technique of crafting bronze statuary in ancient Greece.

There I saw a familiar face at a nearby reading table. With his thinning red hair, ruddy complexion, and acne-scared face, Sinclair Lewis was easy to recognize. He might have been considered homely until he began to talk. Then his face transformed into character and animation, which made all the difference. Writing furiously on a pad, he didn't notice me until I tapped his shoulder.

"Hello, Red."

"Tokol? Never expected to see you in a library."

"I make allowances for literature once in a while. I'm thinking about writing a novel of my own."

"What about?"

"Evil."

"Terrific idea for a book. Wish I'd thought of that."

Lewis and his wife, Dorothy Thompson, the columnist, had recently bought an expansive mock-Tudor in Bronxville, an affluent village just above the city line.

I scooted into an empty chair next to him, both of us speaking in the hushed tones expected of a library. He was still intoxicated, in more ways than one, after winning the Nobel Prize.

"I figured you'd be home slaving on a new book, Red."

"Had to get out of the house. Dotty and me… Sometimes I can't take her know-it-all nag, nag, nagging, always after me about my drinking. Why does she think I drink in the first place?"

"I thought she was still in Berlin covering the Reich for

the *Trib*."

"Naw, the Nazis just gave her the boot. I've always said that if I divorce her, I'd name Hitler as co-respondent."

"May I ask what you're working on?"

"A novel about a right-wing demagogue who becomes president after promising prosperity and greatness, but turns America into a fascist dictatorship."

I chuckled. "Thank god, it can't happen here."

"Say, that's a great title for my book! I just might use it."

We said our goodbyes, and as I left the reading room, I saw Red surreptitiously drink from a small silver flask he had secreted in his coat pocket.

I thought I'd given myself sufficient cover.

I was misguided.

Intending to check for messages at my Chrysler building office, I neared Lex and 42nd just as a black Packard Twelve sedan roared around the corner, and thugs wielding Chicago typewriters opened fire from both front and back passenger windows. I dived under a parked Studebaker as bullets sprayed the air like silver locusts, honeycombing my temporary sanctuary. I heard the Packard's rubber screech to a stop and back up so the assassins could authenticate their kill. With visions of Bonnie and Clyde, I somersaulted into a Rexall, shoved my way through the astonished patrons, and escaped through the loading dock.

The Man With Two Faces had tried to kill me and failed. This time.

I needed a hideout and fast.

It wasn't feasible to return to my room at the Y, and it was possible I'd been linked to Diana. So afraid of compromising her by going to her place, I grabbed a cab to 33 Riverside Drive overlooking the Hudson where Ira and George Gershwin shared adjoining seventeenth-floor penthouses.

Ira, eyes bulging behind his rimless glasses, met me after I was ushered in by Frank, the uniformed doorman, whose wife's hospital bills I had recently paid. The brothers were holding a party, and several of their celebrity guests hovered around a piano where George was tinkling "Someone to Watch Over Me."

I knew the song. Ira had written the verse to George's melody for their musical *Oh Kay*.

Ira said to me, "You're out of breath and, my word, Tokol, you're awfully disheveled. And where did you get that putrid, moth-eaten coat? Looks like you took it off some bum."

"You don't know the half of it, Ira."

"Come have a scotch and tell me about it."

George took his hand off the keys long enough to wave to me. I waved back.

"Ira, I need a place to crash. Just until the Baer-Carnera fight. Some people are after me, but it's all a misunderstanding."

"That's mashugana."

"I know, but I'll resolve it. May I flop on your sofa?"

"Of course, Tokol. I'm aware of what you did for our doorman Frank so if there's anything I can do—"

"Dammit, Ira, no one's supposed to know about Frank."

"Word gets around. You can't keep secrets in New York."

Already I was learning just how prescient Ira was.

I spotted Groucho among the guests. When George finished playing to a round of applause, the Marx brother, wagging his cigar, joined Ira and me.

I said, "Groucho, you appear to be getting younger every day."

"A man's only as old as the woman he feels," he replied.

"In fact, I was telling Ruth the other day that I wished she'd keep my hands to herself."

Ruth was a former chorus girl, now Groucho's wife.

"And how *is* Ruth?" I asked.

"She talks a lot. I've always thought that women should be obscene and not heard."

"Domestic problems?"

"You can say that again. When she accused me of kissing the maid, I told her I was just whispering in her mouth." Groucho took a bow. "Gentlemen, I've had a wonderful evening. But this wasn't it."

I had heard all of Groucho's jokes before, but every time he told them again they were just as funny. After Groucho made his exit, Ira, concerned look on his face, spoke to me in low tones.

"Tokol, you're not going to endanger George and me, are you?"

"Nothing like that, Ira. I just need to lay low."

"Have you read about this Murder Incorporated? What about Machine Gun Kelly, Pretty Boy Floyd, Baby Face Nelson—and those dreadful Italians who are in something called the Mafia? And that awful Meyer Lansky. I went to shul with him!"

"Nothing like that. Just someone with a personal grievance. I'll see to it nothing happens to you and George."

"We're about to move to Hollywood, the two of us. George is going to write scores for the movies. He's got years and years of music in his head."

As I tossed and turned on Ira's sofa overnight, the words to "Someone to Watch Over Me" kept floating through my brain. Who wrote that song anyway?

I needed weaponry, so the following morning I thought

of Gagliano's Pawnshop in East Harlem. The shop was legit. Almost.

I left the Gershwins' building heavily disguised, thanks to doorman Frank, who gave me his extra uniform, hat, and eyeglasses. Peeking into the lobby mirror after pasting my trusty auxiliary mustache on my upper lip, I saw that I resembled a cast member in the *H.M.S Pinafore.*

Pawnbrokers, evidenced by the three gold balls dangling over their doors, have a noble history dating to fifth-century China. But Gaetano Gagliano's on East 105th was more than a lending service for desperate Depression victims needing quick cash. The unassuming Gaetano, balding, glasses thick as Mason jars, was a powerful sub-boss in the Luciano Crime Family, which had Manhattan, The Bronx, Brooklyn, and Jersey in the palm of its black hand.

He and I had a past. During the Castellammarese Wars, I saved his life, a mere trifle on my part and not worth describing here, but Gaetano had never forgotten. In my business, it was useful to have pals on both sides of the law.

Better than a bank, Gaetano also offered an excellent dirty-money laundry service.

When I entered his shop—cluttered with Victrolas, Kodaks, ukuleles, René Lalique stemware, Shirley Temple dolls, a baseball bat signed by Lou Gehrig, and a trumpet once owned by Bunny Berigan—he didn't recognize me at first.

"*Ciao*, Tokol. In that uniform you look like an admiral about to go down with his ship."

"Gotta watch my ass, Gaetano, if you catch my drift."

"I've been there, *amico*. What's on your mind? Say, I got this twenty-four karat gold ring that just came in. Only worn for an hour. She's a beauty. Perfect for that lady of yours. It's yours for a song. In fact, it's yours without a song."

"I need a small arsenal, something I can carry in, say, that alligator-hide suitcase over there."

"Follow me."

He led me to the cellar where he unbolted a sliding door to reveal an impressive armory.

"Just got a new shipment of these Thompson model 1921A SMGs with fifty-round drums and unlimited .45 ACP cartridges, plus optional violin cases with velvet linings."

"Perfect."

He also had Colt M1911.45 semi-automatics, Browning automatic rifles, 12-gauge sawed-off and pump-action shotguns, Smith and Wesson .38 specials, even those cute little Colt Police Positive short .32s for close-up work. As well as German stick grenades and Mills fragmentation No. 23 bombs left over from the Great War.

I filled the alligator.

"*Arrivederci, amico,*" he said. "You got my number."

I left Gaetano's confident I had enough firepower to get me through.

At a corner phone booth I dialed Diana's BUtterfield 8 number, but it wasn't her who answered.

Said the voice on the far end, "Diana's not available, Tokol. Mind if I call you that? It's how you refer to yourself these days, is it not?"

The Man With Two Faces.

"I've been looking all over town for you," he said.

"Where's Diana, dammit?"

"Safe enough. Had to give her pet king cobra some knock-out drops, however."

"How did you find her?"

"A little arm twisting here, leg twisting there. Besides, who but you would call your business Tokoloshe and Son—and all that infers? It's listed in the phone book, for Christ's sake. If you had used your given name you couldn't have revealed yourself better."

"So you put two and two together and came up with me."

"Did you forget we were in Africa together? And that memorable night in Macau..."

"Okay, you win, you bastard. What exactly do you want?"

"You, of course. You took something of irreplaceable value from me. Diana goes free when I have you. An even exchange."

"Where?"

"The Glad Tidings Tabernacle on West Thirty-third Street. It'll have a nice crowd. Aimee Semple McPherson has brought her Foursquare Gospel revival to New York, and the faithful are clamoring to be led to Jesus. My associates and I will be among the throng, along with your Diana. As soon as you step forward after answering Sister McPherson's call to be saved, we'll snatch you and release her."

"Then what?"

"I'll have you exactly where I want you."

Diabolical. I'd be surrounded by assassins in a house of worship.

While Aimee preached to the devout, penned pious sermons, and composed sacred hymns, she was also an oft-married, goodtime gal who wore flashy dresses, fox furs, and made the society pages. Patronizing speakeasies and nightclubs, Aimee drank only water—she claimed. Who would dispute such a cute apostle of the Lord?

However, I knew something Janus didn't.

I was intimately acquainted with America's most famous radio evangelist.

We had been lovers.

It happened when I was on a secret assignment to Los Angeles. Aimee and I fell into a romantic entanglement we imagined was love. Abruptly, she abandoned her Pentecostal notions, I my paganism, and we secretly eloped to an adobe shack in the Arizona desert. There we sated our voracious appetites, performing acts no god worth his salt would approve of, assuming gods have salt.

It was presumed Aimee had drowned while swimming at Venice Beach—until phony ransom demands started pouring in. Suspicions arose.

Five weeks after her disappearance, she returned to her Angelus Temple in Echo Park with a murky cover story that she'd been chloroformed by a mysterious couple called Steve and Rose. Somehow she escaped her kidnappers and walked twenty miles across the blistering desert to safety.

In truth, she and I had decided that lust was not love, so we called it *fini*. I dropped her off at a phone booth in Douglas.

After all the years, however, we remained chummy.

Aimee's gospel road shows were avidly attended, and The Glad Tidings Tabernacle overflowed with the unswerving faithful. Thousands wanting a direct line to the Big Guy Upstairs were turned away, and the cops had to cordon off the streets to contain the hordes.

I entered the edifice through the back in the guise of a uniformed fire marshal there to enforce the safety rules. Through a peephole near the organist I could observe both stage and audience, but the place was so packed, I couldn't spot Diana or The Man With Two Faces. But they were there someplace.

The revival was being broadcast on a nationwide hookup by Aimee's Los Angeles station KFSG. As always, she began by speaking in tongues, the indecipherable glossolalia all believers knew were the very utterances of God, although not even the most righteous understood what the hell her words meant—or if they were words.

Then, in her plain Canadian English, Sister Aimee said into her microphone, "Brothers and sisters, it's now the moment for those who have not found Christ to step forward and be saved."

Instantly, hundreds of worshipers rose, only to be held back by Aimee's deputies brandishing billy clubs.

"I shall recite the name of the first to come forth and discover the Lord. I call on… Diana Dryad."

A murmur from the crowd.

"Is Diana Dryad in the congregation?"

"I'm here, Sister Aimee! Blessed Mother of God."

Wedged between two hulking gorillas rose a diminutive woman garbed in black with a hood that all but hid her face.

"Advance, Diana Dryad, and lead the others who wish to be saved. Praise Jesus."

Diana wriggled from the grasp of the befuddled stooges and led the believers, surging, to the pulpit, where she repented, was sprinkled with holy water, blessed by Sister Aimee, found the Lord, and most important fell into my red-uniformed arms.

Janus had been foiled again.

And I never fired a shot.

Diana and I made our escape in a waiting hook and ladder, and flew in a double-winged Curtiss Goshawk to the Berkeley-Carteret Hotel in Asbury Park. There we registered under assumed names to chart our next move.

Diana needed to do one thing, however. Phone her staff to tell them to feed her king cobra. When Kyle got cranky without his daily ration of mouse, toad, and canary no one was safe, particularly radio script writers.

Over a breakfast of Wheaties and Champagne, she said to me, "When we get to the Bowl for the Baer-Carnera fight—"

"We?"

"After all this, you don't think I'm going to let you go alone, do you? The arena holds tens of thousands. How can you possibly find The Man With Two Faces by yourself?"

"I know each of his faces better than my own. There's a good side and a bad side, and both are indelibly etched into my brain."

"But—"

"In any event, he'll be at ringside while I'll have a vantage point from *in* the ring."

"You mean—"

"Yeah, dollface, I'll be Max Baer's second cornerman."

I knew how to pull strings, one of which was attached to a certain La Cosa Nostra sub-boss in East Harlem with connections.

The open-air Madison Square Garden Bowl was a sprawling mess of an arena at Long Island Boulevard and 48th. It was built on the cheap with sagging, splintery bleachers and a lingering odor of fumes from the regular midget auto races. There was nothing lovely about it, but boxing wasn't lovely either.

Heavyweight champ Primo Carnera was six-feet-six inches, two hundred seventy-five pounds. Born in Italy, he consumed for breakfast a quart of juice, two quarts of milk, twenty pieces of toast, fifteen eggs, a loaf of bread, and half a pound of Virginia ham. The year before, he killed Erie Schaff in the ring.

Happy-go-lucky contender Max Baer was six-feet-two inches, two hundred twenty-one pounds. Born in Nebraska, he took the mail-order Charles Atlas bodybuilding course. Four years earlier he killed Frankie Campbell in the ring.

At the weigh-in, Max plucked hairs from Primo's chest while reciting, "He loves me, he loves me not."

The Clown Prince amused everybody but those he slugged.

Disguised as a has-been, broken-down palooka, with a paste-on flattened nose and stick-on cauliflower ears, I took seriously my role as one of Max's cornerman. But even as I tended to my duties in the ring, armed-packed case at my side, my eyes swept the bleachers for The Man With Two Faces.

So far, no go.

But I spotted Diana, who gave me a thumbs up. She was seated next to her chum Edward, Prince of Wales, and his gal-pal Wallis Warfield, both disguised as hick tourists from Iowa.

Near ringside flitted a cigar-chewing, casual pal of mine toting a huge Speed Graphic. Weegee worked as a darkroom technician for ACME Newspictures, but was hoping to make it big as a tabloid crime photographer. For Weegee there was no such thing as too much gore.

And there was the panhandling Bohemian poet Max Bodenheim and his wife Minna. Never thought I'd ever see Max at a boxing match. How the hell did he even afford a ticket? I liked his poem about Death's voice being like jewels dropped into a satin bag—but it didn't pay the rent. I should have staked him to the bout, but, well, you get busy trying to avoid getting killed.

Despite his more than fifty-pound disadvantage, Max came out slugging in the first round, decking the champ with a hard right, then a series of punches that downed Primo twice more. At the bell, Carnera was so groggy he didn't know which quarter of the ring was his.

I placed Max's stool in his corner, cleaned his mouthpiece, held up his spit bucket, and put an icepack on his neck.

And then I saw him, The Man With Two Faces, sitting close to ringside

Assuming he'd be surrounded by his goons, I figured a little collateral damage wouldn't be a bad thing. I could open fire and in the panic and confusion make it to safety. As I was about to unlatch the suitcase and let fly with my Chicago organ grinder, I realized Janus was seated with Mayor Fiorello La Guardia, reformer Samuel Seabury, Postmaster General James Farley, Labor Secretary Frances Perkins, and Supreme Court Justice Louis Brandeis. I couldn't fire at Janus without taking out the cream of the New Deal.

Damn.

I had to bide my time.

Max tried to finish Primo off in the second round, but, due to his bulk, Carnera absorbed the blows like a bass drum.

At the end of the fifth, as I sponged his kisser with cold water and the cutman closed a few lacerations with an adrenaline-soaked swab, Max wheezed, "I feel like I'm either beatin' a country ham or a dead horse."

As the sweat-drenched rounds careened on, the two fighters clinched like lovers at a prom, wrestled, plunged to the floor, staggered like drunks. Primo, teetering, managed a few solid punches, but it was Max's fusillades of lefts and rights, rights and lefts that created the carnage.

It wasn't until the eleventh that the referee stopped the match.

Max was declared the new heavyweight champ.

The cheering crowd leaped to their feet and I completely lost sight of The Man With Two Faces.

I blew it. Diana was right. She had warned me the crowds

would get in my way.

As the flash guns popped and the horde roared, Max was packed off to his dressing room by his adoring fans, while I, pushed to the rear, struggled to follow, encumbered by Max's stool and the other tools of the cornerman's trade, not to mention my arsenal-filled alligator.

The Man With Two Faces had outfoxed me, just as I had given him the slip at Glad Tidings Tabernacle.

But I never got to Max's dressing room.

In a reeking, urine-stained labyrinth under the bleachers I was snatched by half a dozen or more gorillas, relieved of my case, and dragged to a remote corner of the arena, which was strategically partitioned from view. I must have blacked out because when I came to I found myself upside down strapped to a door-sized sheet of plywood.

"We meet in the flesh once again," said The Man With Two Faces. He sat in front of me on Max's corner stool. "Surprised?"

"Nothing you do surprises me, Janus."

"Did you think your disguise as a punch-drunk cornerman had me fooled, Tokol? You knew I wouldn't miss this fight, and I knew you knew it, although you didn't know I knew it. Plus I was sure you wouldn't try anything, ah, foolish as long as I sat with the imbecile La Guardia and those New Dealers. At heart you were always a softie."

"I don't have to ask what you're going to do to me."

"As I observe you dangling there so unceremoniously, I'm tempted to let my boys use you as a punching bag. But there've been enough blows thrown in this decrepit coliseum tonight. I'm going to do something far more clever."

On a folding table next to him, he opened a familiar case. Even while hanging upside down, I saw clearly it was the valise he carried in Africa, Macau, and, significantly, Singapore. It contained his polished, keen-edge single-piece throwing knives.

"Remember when, plastered, you distracted me while I was throwing, Tokol? How you made me lose my aim? How the love of my life was suddenly removed from me? All because of you."

"She was my love too, you bastard, and because of your stupid mistake she was also my loss."

He picked up one of his knives and flicked the tip with his finger.

"I'm not going to miss this time, Tokol, nor shall I attempt a silhouette. Eleven of these knives, finest Damascus steel on earth, are about to make a neat diamond-shaped pattern in your upper torso, with the twelfth to enter right between your eyes."

"Um, Janus, let's not be hasty. Why don't we talk this over? There's lots of stuff we could do together for old time's sake. Remember how grand it was when we were slaughtering Berber tribesmen in Morocco? Let's grab a few beers at Jack and Charlie's 21. Take in a show. Cole Porter's *Anything Goes* is at the Alvin. Palisades Park just got a new Cyclone roller coaster."

"That's all shit, Tokol, and you know it. The moment for talking has passed. Now it's merely a matter of mass times velocity."

He stepped back.

"Eighteen feet?" I said.

"Ah, you remember. The perfect distance between hand and target."

A full-spin thrower, he always used a hammer grip. Preferred his throws to be direct and clean. Conscious, of course, of wind and air resistance.

I was about to become a bloody pincushion.

He took his usual stance, left foot forward, which I had watched him do hundreds of times before, but never were his knives directed at me.

"One."

He raised his throwing arm, the first knife in his customary grip.

"Two."

His wrist cocked in precise position.

"Thr—"

He never completed the word as his mouth gaped, his eyes taking on an amazed expression. He never knew what hit him.

But I did. A dart protruding from the center of his forehead. He collapsed, dropping the knife, which clanged on the cement.

I heard shouts and shots, the rattle of tommies, screams and cries.

The next thing I knew I was hauled off the board, my straps removed, and in Diana's arms.

"His, his goons?" I stuttered.

"Taken care of, Tokee, darling. All of them. Relax. Your friends are here."

"Friends?"

"You didn't think I was going to let you do this thing alone, did you? You were bait, and Janus fell for it."

Then I saw Diego Rivera blowing the smoke from the barrel of his pistol. Gaetano Gagliano with some of his Mafioso brothers shouldering Browning automatics. Aimee McPherson held a Colt short 32. Frank, Ira's doorman, lugged a pump-action shotgun. Groucho wielded a 12-gauge sawed-off.

Even Sinclair Lewis was there with a Smith and Wesson .38.

"Red," I said to Lewis, "never thought I'd see you in a place like this."

"There may be a novel in it, Tokol."

"And you," I said to Diana. "You pinged Janus with your blowgun."

"And obviously, I got the right face. The poison worked just as the Waorani tribesmen showed me when I was a little girl in the Amazon. They knew a lot for naked people."

"But... poison?"

"From my pet cobra. Kyle gets off on being milked. Why did you think I adopted him in the first place? Oh, lookee, I think your friend with the two faces is still breathing." She put her ear close to his mouth. "My mistake. Poison works even faster than I thought."

"How did you—"

"I had a feeling he would pull something like this, and that he was more likely to find you than you him. Darling, I knew you'd never listen. It was merely a matter of our keeping you in our sight after the fight, allowing his hoods to snatch you, and then coming to the rescue deus ex machina—just like the cavalry in those adorable Hoot Gibson Westerns."

There was some cleanup we had to do at the Madison Square Garden Bowl, little things such as disposing of the bodies, after which we took a breather, the three of us.

Diana, Kyle, and I.

In Diana's penthouse, surrounded by her collection of Georgia O'Keeffe abstractions, sculptures, and ceramics, we savored romantic evenings with pitchers of martinis and Twinkies—while through the Zenith Stratosphere the crooner Russ Columbo sang "Prisoner of Love" on the Blue Network.

Until...

Good evening, Mr. and Mrs. America and all the ships at sea. Let's go to press. Flash! New York City police have discovered a gangland boneyard in an East River lot near the Madison Square Garden Bowl in Long Island City. Seven unidentified corpses were unearthed, all riddled with gunshot wounds. This may be the beginning of a new war among the Mafia families.

Hmmm. Strange. I thought I counted eight corpses, including Janus.

Flash! New York isn't the only bed of organized crime activity. From Minnesota comes word of a violent underworld enterprise known as the Syndicate. This reporter has learned exclusively that a certain acquaintance, who from now on shall be known only as, well, Certain Acquaintance, plans to risk his life by single-handedly bringing down this unholy alliance of criminals. Good luck, C.A.

...For Jergens Lotion, this is Walter Winchell wishing you lotions of love.

two

Po-lice and Vigilantes 1935

I'd barely gotten over the death of my pal Lawrence of Arabia when I received more lousy news.

An acquaintance of mine, a newspaper guy named Leon Linquist, called collect from Minneapolis to say he was in trouble with the mop. *Mop?* Damned line was all noise.

Such distractions only added to my foul mood. True, I was no longer under threat by The Man With Two Faces. I had seen his corpse in a shallow grave in some crummy Queens lot. But it was T.E. Lawrence's death in a motorcycle crack-up in Dorset, England, that hit me hard. To me, Lawrence was simply known as Ned, and I'd befriended him well before Lowell Thomas. Not that I was envious of the unctuous NBC Radio commentator, but Thomas crudely capitalized on his shallow relationship with Lawrence, while I hadn't— wouldn't. Lowell even published a book about Ned stuffed with errors and exaggerations. And I wasn't mentioned once.

But, thankfully, Thomas wasn't around to describe that delightfully sordid occasion at the Baron Hotel in Aleppo when Ned and I stripped to our loins in a drunken romp that neither of us regretted. Ned was short, barely five-feet-five and self-conscious about his height, yet he made up for it by good living, a teetotaler, mostly, and a vegetarian who abstained from tobacco. He tested himself by periodically fasting and dehydrating himself.

Ned was a decade older than me, educated at Oxford, and at first I saw him more as a mentor and big brother than as an intimate. That quickly changed, and he became especially alluring after the Arabs put a price on his head.

He was fascinated by me and *my* upbringing as well.

"Tell me more about Kansas, Tokol," he once said after an afternoon of passion.

"You're joking."

"I've never been to your prairies."

"I can't tell if you're being facetious or just batty."

"I have the same problem."

I loved fondling his flesh, which was so much softer than one would expect of a man accustomed to desert heat and sand. In our intimacies, I was startled by his advocacy of the riding crop, which he insisted be applied to him in pleasure.

"Again, Tokol," he would say, "Again."

Ned professed to his friends that he had no interest in sex, while believing in the honesty of perfect love.

I can state with absolute authority that Lawrence of Arabia believed in both.

We once enjoyed carnal knowledge, the two of us, on the hump of a camel, awkwardly yet triumphantly. Years later, he and I shared laughs over it in Ankara while guzzling too many glasses of arak.

I was in my sixty-third floor office suite in the Chrysler Building brooding while studying the sun sliding below the Hudson, pinpoints of lights from the myriad buildings multiplying throughout the metropolis, making the city seem more beautiful than it was. There's little uglier than the sight of hungry men and women waiting in a breadline.

I'd elected to stay in while Diana attended the premier of a new Blue Network show, "The Chase and Sanborn Potpourri Hour" starring Edgar Bergen and Charlie McCarthy, Ed Wynn, Jimmy Durante, Jane Froman, the Boswell Sisters, and Phil Spitalny and His All-Girl Orchestra.

"In good conscience, I can't miss that show, Tokee, darling. Or should I call you C.A. from now on?" She chuckled. "Anyway, the show's to be a live remote from the Hippodrome Theatre. Plus I'll be able to wear my pearls, diamond tiara, and chinchilla stole."

As writer of record of radio's most popular daytime serials, Diana had to go, but I had no interest radio joie de vivre, intending to sack out on my office couch rather than my bare room at the Y. While the famous Lavender Star of Africa diamond heist left me impossibly rich, allowing me to indulge in various challenging amusements, I was essentially an ascetic. Like a cat I slept about anywhere.

Linquist's call from Minnesota interrupted my reflections about Lawrence and our exploits in Aqaba during Allenby's Ottoman campaign.

"Leon," I growled into the phone, "your line stinks. Long distance is expensive. No wonder you called collect."

"You can afford it, Tokol."

"How'd you get this number anyway?"

"From Winchell."

Of course, Walter, the blabbermouth. Linquist, Winchell, and I were mutual acquaintances. Rarely did a week go by that I didn't huddle with the commentator at the Stork Club's Table 50. Up to now, our arrangement to exchange mutually advantageous information suited us both. Winchell, who was now referring to me on the air as Certain Acquaintance — or C.A. — had mentioned that Linquist might be calling, and I'd forgotten.

"Tell me again," I said to Leon. "You're in trouble with

the *mop*?"

"Mob, Tokol, mob. Racketeers. Thugs. Four of them disguised as New Deal Democrats nearly beat me to a pulp. In broad daylight. Threatened my life, my family's."

"You went to the police?"

"That's a laugh. The Minneapolis cops are in on it. Now I carry a pistol. Then they tried to frame me by claiming I sodomized a sixteen-year-old hooker because I happened to stay in the same hotel where she serviced her johns. The little bitch had been paid off, but she plainly perjured herself in court, so I beat the rap."

"Why are they so pissed off at you?"

"Because my *Prairie Patriot* tells the truth about the Syndicate and corruption and graft. You won't believe what I have on the governor, a bribable bum named Karlson."

"Sounds serious, Leon."

"They've put out a contract on me, whatever that means, although I've a pretty good idea."

I met Linquist when I was on a job that took me to neighboring St. Paul, and we hit it off.

The FBI's Hoover had begged me to help bust the Alvin Karpis-Arthur Barker Gang, headed by Barker's mom Kate, better known as Ma. They'd snatched St. Paul banker Edward Bremer, and were holding him for a two-hundred-thousand dollar ransom. Working with Special Agent Mike Litvak, I arranged for the ransom's delivery and Bremer's freedom, but the gang escaped. Litvak, a likeable moron, was responsible, but I took the fall. At least we got the kidnap victim back.

Now, I had good intelligence the gang was hiding out in Florida. I intended to deal with them after I finished my current assignment.

As for Linquist, he fought for principles. Therefore, Leon

was as poor as I was wealthy. I was occasionally for sale—depending on the cause—and he wasn't, which is why I admired his passion. For me crime fighting was more of a hobby.

"What do you want me to do, Leon? I'm in Manhattan. Have a business to run. Gotta leave for Louisiana tomorrow."

"I know where you are, Tokol, and I'm aware of what you do. That's why I called. I need you in Minneapolis before something happens to me."

Tokoloshe and Son Cleansing Services was used to cleaning up crap, of course, never with feather dusters or floor brushes, but sometimes I spread myself too thin. Occasionally, I wished I actually had a son, making it a true family business.

"Leon, you can't afford me."

"Listen, Tokol, I've got fourteen-hundred bucks in the bank. Take it all plus the title to my newspaper. I also have a wife and a nine-year-old daughter. They've got to account for something. Like your conscience."

I sighed. "Okay, but tomorrow I'm on the train to New Orleans where I intend to buy a six-cylinder DeSoto Airstream and drive it up to Baton Rouge. After that, Diana and I need to see some guy in a place called Pampa, Texas. When we're finished we'll head to Minneapolis."

"It may be too late by then."

"I can work just so many miracles, Leon."

The next afternoon, Diana saw me off at McKim, Mead, and White's grand Pennsylvania Station where I was to catch the Pennsy to connect to the Southern Railroad's Crescent Limited. I shuddered in humility each time I entered that magnificent Beau Arts cathedral to railroading, knowing it would forever endure—like the Great Pyramid of Giza.

On the congested platform, Diana said, "Tokee, darling, I do wish I could go with you, but my scribes are so far behind with "Our Gal Zelda" and "When a Widow Weds," I must stay here to whip them into action. If I lose Proctor & Gamble we'll go off the air. I'll catch up with you in Texas after you finish your work in Baton Rouge."

"But Pampa's in the Dust Bowl, dollface. It's a cataclysm out there. So why—"

"No time to explain now. I'll wire you before I leave."

Meeting lips, we embraced, and then I swung aboard the Pullman. In my compartment, as the romantic countryside of Bayonne, Perth Amboy, and Carteret flashed by, I open my valise and inspected the blowback semi-automatic revolver I obtained from Gaetano Gagliano, who was like a father to me.

Peering through glasses slightly thicker than jelly jars, Gagliano had said, "I got what you wanted, Tokol, a 7.65-millimeter Browning, but it don't have much stopping power. Here's a better choice. This Walther PP. It was removed from the corpse of an unfortunate gent from Palermo before he had a chance to fire it."

"I already pack a Smith and Wesson M&P .38 Special, Gaetano. No, it's the Browning I want. Compact, light, cheap, and perfect for an amateur."

"But *you* ain't no amateur."

"It's the world's deadliest handgun."

"Whad'ya mean?"

"The Browning 7.65 was used to assassinate Archduke Ferdinand in Sarajevo, setting off the Great War, which murdered over thirty-five-million people. If it can do that, I figure it'll serve me just as good. Your Browning may not be the original, which is in Vienna's Museum of Military History, along with Ferdinand's Graf and Stift touring car, but—"

"No, no Tokol. It *is* the original."

"Huh?"

"I had it stolen from the museum. Yeah, *amico*, it's the very gun that killed Archduke Ferdinand. Anything for you."

"Gaetano..."

"You saved my life once. Least I could do."

The Pennsy got me to DC, where I changed to the Crescent Limited to New Orleans. In my compartment, I cleaned, oiled, and wrapped the Browning in tissue with a neat bow, appreciative of its lethal place in history. Then I headed to the dining car to enjoy the potage paysanne, roast guinea with currant jelly, hearts of romaine, and fresh plum tarte, after which I relaxed with a few glasses of Dewar's single malt while reading F. Scott Fitzgerald's *Taps at Reveille*.

Within two days I was in Baton Rouge, where I parked my new DeSoto Airstream, and gazed up at the Louisiana State Capitol building, thirty-four stories, built just two years before as a limestone monument to the former governor, now senator, Huey Long.

Which was why I was there.

On the drive up the Mississippi to Baton Rouge, I heard Huey rage through the Airstream's staticky Motorola:

They say I'm ignorant, and I am, on account of I got no education. But I'm a lot smarter than all them SOBs put together when I say: Every man a king, every man a king, but no one wears a crown. I can scare or buy ninety-nine out of every one-hundred men, and then I can't can go to hell 'cause all I cares about is the boys at the fork of the creeks.

To the rich, Share-the-Wealth Huey was an amoral demagogue—but he was a hero to the poor, promoting a scheme to guarantee an annual income for every breathing American. Disguised fascism, his critics called it. Surrounded by a thug contingent, Huey ran Louisiana as his personal fiefdom. He called himself the Kingfish after the con man on radio's *Amos 'n' Andy.*

This year would prove to be a bad one for Long, often described as the most dangerous man in America. And I would be partly responsible.

On the dot I was ushered into the office of Carl Weiss, MD, on the seventh floor of the Reymond Building. The ear, nose, and throat specialist's credentials were impeccable. A Tulane graduate, he studied in Austria, interned at New York's Bellevue, headed the Louisiana Medical Society, and was a Kiwanis in good standing.

"We meet again, Dr. Weiss," I said.

"Did you bring what you said you'd bring, Mr. Tokoloshe?"

Weiss was all business.

"You could have bought one of these in a local five-and-dime, doctor. In the South it's easier to buy a howitzer than a quart of hooch."

"I needed something untraceable."

"Here it is, wrapped with a pretty red bow. Plus a box of .32-caliber tin-plated, copper-jacketed bullets. Suggest you practice shooting at soup cans before putting it to actual use."

"I'm not unfamiliar with guns, Mr. Tokoloshe. This is Louisiana after all."

I turned to leave. Then, "Doctor, I remain prepared to do the deed myself, which was why I was handsomely paid by your associates."

"It's something I must do on my own. A matter of principle and pride. Huey Long undermined the judicial career of my father-in-law. Claims my wife has negro blood, which in Louisiana is unthinkable. He has destroyed my family."

The doc spewed a litany of other grievances.

I had some reservations about leaving that historic,

earth-shattering Browning in the hands of a greenhorn, but the customer's always right—unless he gets me killed.

Before I crossed into Texas, I phoned Leon Linquist to inquire if he was still alive.

"But for how long I don't know, Tokol. Ever hear of a mobster known as Hyman Cherry Lips Zwillman? No? Remember the name in case I go down before you get here. Bastard runs the Syndicate in the Twin Cities. When are you arriving anyway?"

"Patience, Leon. Don't leave the house. Bolt the doors, lock the windows."

"Easy for you to say. I've got a paper to run."

Next I phoned Diana's BUtterfield 8 number, simple to remember since some writer named O'Hara just published a book of that title.

"Finished in Baton Rouge already, Tokee, darling?"

"It was a cinch. A mere advisory role. Meet me at Love Field in Dallas."

"I'll wire you my ETA in care of Western Union. Howard's already in Brooklyn. We're flying out of Floyd Bennett Field."

Howard Hughes had just broken the record for the fastest flight in aviation history, three-hundred-fifty-two miles an hour. When not amusing himself piloting the planes in his vanity air force, he made both movies and movie starlets.

I tolerated Howard, although he was starting to get weird. I wouldn't put it past him if he put the make on Diana.

Listening to the Airstream's Motorola en route to Texas, I heard the stunning news that G-men had gunned down Ma Barker and one of her sons, Fred, in a house at Lake Weir, Florida. Sonofabitch. The paunchy prick J. Edgar beat me to 'em. But all was not lost. Ma's son Arthur and his pal Alvin Karpis were still at large.

I had dibs on them. My prey.

Karpis had just been named Public Enemy Number One. I intended to redeem myself.

Parking the DeSoto at the edge of Love Field, I watched Hughes and Diana swoop in on Howard's new open-cockpit H-X Racer, beautiful, metallic, sleek. Diana, sexy in flight suit and goggles, bussed me, but when I reached to shake Howard's hand he shrank away.

"Always consider hygiene, Tokol. Never touch another's hands—unless they belong to Katharine Hepburn. Even then… Bathe four times a day, always with oodles of lather. And use separate bars of soap."

He was phobic about germs, so I wondered how he ever managed sex. But he had good teeth.

"How was your flight?" I asked.

"Four-hours, eleven minutes, seventeen seconds. But I'll do better. I'm designing a new baby to fly around the world in record time. Wiley Post, may he rest in peace, set the record two years ago: seven days, eighteen hours, forty-nine minutes in a Lockheed Vega. I intend to do it in less than five days—now that my competition's been eliminated."

The one-eyed Post and his passenger Will Rogers had just been killed in a crash in Alaska.

"When are you heading back to Hollywood, Howard."

"As soon as I fix some glitches on my H-X Racer. Besides, if I stay away too long Kate Hepburn may two-time me with Spencer Tracy."

"Between aviation and Hepburn, you must have your very sanitary hands full."

"I'm filming *Heaven's Devils*, sequel to *Hell's Angels*. I sank just under four million into *Angels* and doubled my investment. So I'm putting five million into *Devils* and bringing back Jean Harlow to star."

"I guess a four million ain't what it used to be."

"Tokol, I always said I'd be the planet's greatest golfer, the top Hollywood film producer, most daring pilot, and the world's richest man. My score's already three out of four."

"Then we need to celebrate by eating barbecue in Dallas. Will you join Diana and me?"

"Okay, but I'm eating only fudge, milk, and water until I get back to my personal chef in California. He's the only one who knows how to cook to my exact specifications. For example, vegetables pared into perfect half-inch squares with each corner precisely cut to a forty-five-degree angle. Nobody else does it right."

After dinner, Diana, Howard, and I repaired to the Magnolia Hotel, former headquarters of Magnolia Petroleum, in downtown Dallas. On the roof, revolving in neon, was Pegasus, the flying red horse. Our rooms, known as the Petroleum Suite, were decorated with images of oil drills, derricks and pumpjacks, all appearing phallic and masculine.

It was obvious Diana had a crush on Howard. She was a libertine who never hid her amorous impulses, which I neither encouraged nor discouraged.

Engrossed, I watched as she and the aviator barnstormed on the bed, accomplishing loop-the-loops, barrel rolls, spins, dives, and a few aeronautical maneuvers I never thought possible.

Then Diana, touching a rivulet of sweat on her brow, said, "Come join us, Tokol."

Following that spiritual night, which left our sheets damp and wrinkled, Howard checked out of the Magnolia while I groggily reached Leon Linquist from the house phone.

"I'm being watched, Tokol. I feel it. But I have to get groceries. We're almost out of milk, and we used up all the butter."

"Tighten your belts, Leon. Diana and I will be in Minneapolis within three days."

The state highway was clear as we drove north into the Texas Panhandle, although many of the side roads were nearly impassable, encrusted by drifting sand. Sparse traffic, save for an occasional stripped-down car or beaten-up truck. No greenery, no grass. Even the weeds looked defeated, and the few scraggly trees were leafless. Farms were abandoned, their buildings drab, paint literally sand-blasted off.

The heat was unrelenting.

Once oil-prosperous, the distressed town of Pampa wasn't far from the Oklahoma border. As we pulled into the grungy jerkwater, we were caught in a sudden black blizzard, and I was afraid the billowing dust, which reduced visibility to a few yards, would stall the DeSoto's engine.

"What did you get us into?" I asked Diana.

"Stay cool, Tokee, darling. Just a little dust. Someday the world will thank us for our itty-bitty odyssey. Pull over here."

"A church?"

A sign read FOURSQUARE BAPTIST CALVARY APOSTOLIC CHURCH, and next to it a hand-lettered poster advertising a social with music by the Corn Cob Trio. Obviously, this was one of the few progressive churches in a part of the nation where joy was grudgingly rationed out.

We parked, watching the storm swirl wraith-like around us. Then the wind died and our range of vision improved, but I could feel my teeth crunching on the grains of dust.

"Cover your mouth with your hankie, Tokee, darling, and let's go in."

Three dudes, decked out in showy cowboy suits complete

with chaps and Stetsons, were making noises with fiddle, banjo, and guitar. They sawed and plunked as the dancers, wearing their go-to-meeting duds, hoedowned with an alle- mande left, circle right, promenade all, roll away with a half sashay, and a do-si-do. I felt a little out of place in my corduroy knickers and boots from Fifth Avenue's Best and Company— although, wisely, I left my pith helmet in the car.

"Cole Porter it ain't," I groused to Diana about the music.

"Shush, Tokee. Keep your eye on the guitar player, the one with the cigarette dangling from his lips."

He was a lanky, thin-faced young man with a full head of curly hair. When the Corn Cob Trio took a break, Diana corralled him.

"Mr. Woodrow Wilson Guthrie, I presume?" she said.

"They just calls me Woody, ma'am."

"I'm Miss Dryad from New York and this is my associate, Mr. Tokoloshe."

"Do tell," Woody said, eyeing our Eastern threads.

"Mr.... Ah, Woody, you probably recall a certain Mr. John Lomax?"

"Yep, older fella. Came to Pampa with his kid Alan lug- gin' one of them big electric phonograph recording machines, which musta weighed three-hundred pounds. Claimed he was collectin' music for history. Mr. Lomax had me sing 'bout every damned song I ever knowed, 'cept them I wrote myself. He only wanted the old ones. But y'know, when you think about it, all our songs is just little notes in one great, big song."

"That's what I want to talk to you about, Woody. Are you familiar with the name William S. Paley?"

"Never heard of him."

"Mr. Paley's head of the famous Columbia Broadcasting System, and he wants to sign you to a contract to perform on his network in New York. He just acquired Bing Crosby, Kate Smith, and the Atwater-Kent Orchestra conducted by Josef Pasternack. Mr. Paley heard your Lomax recordings and was impressed."

"Damn, if that ain't somethin'. You mean this here Mr. Paley actually wants me, a fella born in Okemah, Oklahoma, to go all the ways to New York with my git-tar just to sing?"

"Exactly, Woody. You might even live in one of those tall buildings overlooking Central Park."

"And I can sing whatever I cotton to, not just them old square-dance numbers?"

"Mr. Paley wants to hear 'The Bear Went Over the Mountain,' 'Froggy Went A'courtin',' and 'Go Tell Aunt Rhody,' the sorts of folksongs he heard at the Philmont Country Club while growing up on Chadwick Street in Philadelphia. And he'd like you to dress in bib overalls and red flannel shirts, so you look authentic. You'll be a sensation."

"Heck, ma'am, I don't even wear no bib overalls here in dusty Pampa."

"But you're turned out like a cowboy."

"That's 'cause I'm helpin' my two fellow Corn Cobbers, my brother-in-law Matt Jennings and Cluster Baker. Y'see, Miss Dryad, the words is what's important. I gets my ideas out of the Amarillo newspaper, writes down a few lines, then I sing high when everybody else sings low, sing fast when they sings slow, and so I gets myself a new tune."

"Shouldn't you sing what people want?"

"Shucks, I'm out to sing ditties provin' it's the people's world, and that the world's knocked 'em all to heck, which ain't right."

"Woody, I don't think there's a lot of money in the kind of songs you want to sing, protest songs."

"My songs won't get no hugs or kisses from the capitalists. I aim to sing about po-lice and vigilantes, who's carryin' a gun and where the peace is, what it's like to fight the law, people who's been dislocated, the refugees tryin' to get to California, about the poll tax and Jim Crow, the sharecroppers and the coal miners, the union men who heads is busted, the banks and the scabs, the peaches and prunes and pickers, and maybe a little fun song along the way like, 'Jaggy, jaggy, bum, bum / And a hey piggy, run.'"

Diana sighed. "Dear, dear Woody, I suspect you'll never land a gig at El Morocco or the Onyx Club."

"Never heard of them places, Miss Dryad. Besides, anyone who uses more than three chords on a git-tar is just showin' off. I'm plannin' to hitch to California, so you tell your Mr. Paley, thanks but no thanks. If I ever get heard on the radio it'll be on my own terms."

Impulsively, Diana took Woody's hand and kissed him on his whiskery cheek.

"I gotta be driftin' along, Miss Dryad." He tipped his Stetson. "Been good to know you."

Diana and I dined at the town's best and only eatery where the chili was crunchy with grit, and bedded for the night in a grubby boarding house on sheets with the texture of the beach at Galveston. The Panhandle was bone dry—not only because of the drought—so Diana and I finished off the flask I kept in the Airstream's glove compartment. Prohibition still reigned in the Bible Belt.

In the morning we set off for Minnesota.

Conditions worsened as we headed north through Oklahoma, the sun's rays barely penetrating the stifling air, resulting in an unremitting grayness. We drove through ghost towns and empty farms, sagging fences nearly buried under banks of thistles and tumbleweed, fields overrun by grasshoppers and jackrabbits. Then the air began to crackle with static electricity and distant flashes of lightning, and suddenly it poured big pellets of muddy water that pelted the windshield. It was over almost as soon as it began. Too little, too late, too dirty.

As we drove into Kansas City, where we planned to spend the night, we heard on station WDAF that, in a driving rain, a four-year-old chestnut named Omaha won the Belmont Stakes by a length and a half. The third horse to win the legendary Triple Crown.

"I won twenty grand on Omaha," I boasted to Diana.

"Did you, Tokee? I won forty."

The rolling prairie gradually became green and lush as we entered Minnesota, and along the clear streams and rivers were fertile groves of ash, maple, and oak. The farms were tidy and prosperous, and even the cows appeared contented—as though a dust bowl in the heartland never existed.

In Minneapolis, we checked into a suite at the Leamington Hotel on Third Avenue, where I bought a copy of the *Star* and saw a blazing headline followed by a Baton Rouge dateline.

HUEY LONG ASSASSINATED

Intending to intimidate state lawmakers, the Kingfish had gone to the capitol where, in the lobby, Carl Weiss shot him in the gut with a 32-caliber Browning. Huey's cossacks opened fire on Weiss and kept firing even as he lay dead on the marble floor, awash with blood. The doc ended up with more than sixty bullet holes in his body. So many slugs flew it was likely Huey's own guards cut the Kingfish down in the crossfire.

Weiss was a rank amateur after all. If you wanted something done right you had to do it yourself.

Someone, probably one of Huey's skull-crushers, made off with Weiss's Browning, the gun so important to military history.

Leon Linquist, a bitter adversary of both Herbert Hoover and FDR, was an unrepentant Marxist, passionate opponent of American entry into the Great War, and fervent defender of Sacco and Vanzetti. In his *Prairie Patriot*, he inveighed against municipal corruption as well as hanky-panky in his own Farmer-Labor Party. What's worse, he also attacked the racketeers known as the Syndicate. Little wonder he piled up enemies.

When Diana and I pulled up at Leon's home on Second Avenue South in Minneapolis, I wasn't surprised to see a bunch of cops and several prowl cars, dome lights flashing.

I said. "We may be too late."

But then I spotted Leon angrily exchanging words with the cops. As I left my car he saw me and broke away.

"They almost got me, Tokol. As I was getting out of my Ford V-8 in the alley behind the house, a black sedan roared around the corner and someone inside opened fire with a tommy gun. I saw them coming and ducked under my car just in time, but the car's shot to hell."

"I told you to stay inside."

"I had to shop for necessities."

"Any idea who they were?"

"Yeah, it was Cherry Lips Zwillman himself firing the trench sweeper. I'd know his ugly puss anywhere. Naturally, Police Chief Big Tuna Carney says that's bull, that the shooters were racketeers up from Chicago, and I was a case of mistaken identity. He claims Cherry Lips has an iron-clad alibi: he was getting a haircut at his favorite hangout, Toblinsky's Barbershop. Everyone in the Twin Cities knows Cherry Lips has Big Tuna in his pocket, and that they both take orders from Governor Alvin B. Karlson. However, now I've got the goods on 'em, definitive proof. It'll be in my paper tomorrow—if I live that long."

"I think I'll pay a call on Mr. Hyman Cherry Lips Zwillman."

"He's got an office on Hennepin Avenue where he runs his jukebox and gumball businesses, but you're more likely to find him at Toblinsky's on Nicollet Avenue. Isador Toblinsky is better known as Alibi Guy because he's not only Cherry Lips's cover-up man but his chief enforcer. Alibi Guy insists he was trimming Cherry Lips's sideburns at the very moment I was nearly liquidated."

"I'll locate the newly-trimmed Cherry Lips and ask him politely to lay off and let you do your work."

"Being polite's been tried."

"I'm in need of a nice shave in any event. Know any good barbers?"

The next day, I parked on Nicollet and walked into the shop. No customers, save for two goons wearing double-breasteds and hideous ties. Perched on a soapbox was a cherubic, gap-toothed shoeshine boy. All were being entertained by a shawl-draped, heavy-coated old woman playing traditional Yiddish airs on a concertina. I knew the music from my days running guns in the Holy Land, and thought I'd puke if I heard "Hava Nagila" one more time.

The barber approached me, an open straight razor in his hand.

"Help you?"

"Are you Mr. Alibi Guy Toblinsky?"

"Who wants to know?"

"I'm an old pal of Arthur Barker just passing through. Doc

told me anytime I needed a close shave I should see Alibi Guy."

"Pal of Doc's, huh? Say, too bad about his ma, gettin' all shot up like that. Where's he been hidin' anyway?"

"If I told you it might get out to the wrong parties — if you get the idea."

"Take the chair, mister."

Just then Cherry Lips Zwillman walked into the shop. I recognized him from the mug shots Leon showed me. Fat face, receding hairline, flashy three-piece suit. More than a passing resemblance to my favorite romantic screen star: Edward G. Robinson.

"Say, who let her in?" Cherry Lips said, pointing at the old biddy squeezing the concertina. "Get her and that squawk box the hell out."

Alibi Guy said, "Ah, let her stay, Cherry Lips. Reminds me of my grandma. She docked at Ellis Island as an infant and spoke Yiddish and only Yiddish the rest of her life. And she lived to be a hundred."

"Okay, but if she plays 'Hava Nagila' shoot her."

A mobster after my own heart.

When Cherry Lips noticed me reclining in the barber chair, my face lathered, and the boy shining my brogans, he said, "Who the hell are you?"

"Name's, ah, Smith. Out of Detroit."

Alibi Guy said, "He's a pal of Doc Barker."

"Doc, huh? Never did like Barker. Takes too many chances."

I said, "But you gotta cut him a little slack on account of his ma being gunned down. And his brother."

"Yeah, sad day for everyone. Ma was a great woman. She kicked ass."

Cherry Lips went to a pay phone on the wall, dropped in a nickel, and started a conversation I couldn't quite over-hear, except, occasionally, the name of Leon Linquist. Then he flopped into a chair, and began working on the crossword puzzle in the *Star*.

I couldn't resist.

"Hey, Cherry Lips," I said from my reclining position. "Couldn't help hearing you refer to Leon Linquist on the phone."

"What about the prick bastard? And only my pals and my sainted mother call me Cherry Lips."

"Heard there was just a shooting outside Linquist's house."

"Musta been some pros up from Chicago or K.C. So what? Deserves whatever he got."

"They missed."

"Bastard's time will come."

"What have you got against him anyway?"

"Ain't none of your business but I'll tell you. Linquist runs this cheap rag called the *Prairie Patriot* in which he's tryin' to make out that Governor Karlson, Chief Big Tuna Carney, and me is all in the Syndicate, up to our asses in numbers, prosti-tution, loansharkin', and bribery. Hell, nobody's ever proved nothin'."

"Until tomorrow."

"Huh?"

"Linquist is publishing a story he thinks will bust your sad ass for good."

"Say, who the hell are you?" Cherry Lips leaped up, reaching for the gat I knew was in a shoulder holster under his coat. "Get him, boys," he yelled to the two sitting goons. "He ain't one of us."

Suddenly, the old lady began playing "Hava Nagila" at

triple speed.

From under the barber's sheet, where I had surreptitiously positioned my Smith and Wesson, I let go with a shot that winged Cherry Lips in his firing arm. Before I could get off another shot, Alibi Guy spun the barber chair so violently I not only lost my grip on my .38 but now faced the mirror on the wall.

As the two stooges sprang up, guns in their hands, the fossilized concertina lady whipped off her shawl, opened her coat to produce a sawed-off Browning A5 pump action, and cut down the goons.

She was, in disguise, Diana, of course.

Would I have entered a mob hangout without backup?

Although my back was now turned, from my prone position in the barber chair I saw in the mirror the wounded Cherry Lips advancing on me. At the same time, Alibi Guy raised the straight razor, about to slice the blade across my throat. Then the three of us were caught in a sudden death grip: Cherry Lips depositing his heavy torso on top of my chair-bound body while my two hands clutched Alibi Guy's wrist to fend off the razor.

I expected Diana to let loose with the shotgun again, but, locked in a sort of tableau, Cherry Lips, Alibi Guy, and I would all buy the farm if she did. Cherry Lips was too heavy to shake off and I was losing the strength to repel Alibi Guy's razor.

I thought I was a gonner when I heard a puff sound and witnessed the surprised expression on Alibi Guy's mug, although he couldn't see the dart in the middle of his forehead. The razor fell to the floor along with Alibi Guy himself.

"What the hell?" Cherry Lips said, gaping at Diana, for which he was similarly rewarded with a dart between his eyes.

Diana helped roll his big frame off of me and onto the floor.

The poison tip worked swiftly. I'd have to give Kyle a special thanks when I got back to New York.

"Oh, oh," Diana said to me, as she peeled away her old-lady mask. "We have a witness."

The shoeshine kid, eyes wide, mouth open, staring in astonishment at the carnage on the floor.

"What's your name, boy?" I said.

"Elmer."

"Elmer, you only polished one of my brogans. How's about doing the other one before I leave? And don't step in the blood."

"Right away, mister."

"I suspect this barber shop's going to be boarded up for a long time. How'd you like a new job?"

"You betcha."

"Tomorrow, I want you to report to Mr. Leon Linquist at the *Prairie Patriot* on Lake Street. Tell him I sent you. But to anyone else you never saw me."

"Saw who?"

"Elmer, you might become the assistant publisher someday."

The next day Leon's paper had not one but two scoops.

ZWILLMAN AND THREE GANGSTERS
RUBBED OUT BY RIVAL GANG IN BARBER SHOP

PATROIT EXCLUSIVE: ZWILLMAN, CARNEY,
KARLSON DIRECTLY LINKED TO SYNDICATE

A victory for freedom of the press and the rule of law.
The police found no clues as to who actually annulled

Cherry Lips and the others, but they did discover an old concertina someone had abandoned at the scene. Plus odd puncture wounds in the heads of Zwillman and Toblinsky, but no sign of what made them.

"How can I thank you, Tokol?" Linquist told me as we said our goodbyes. "I wish I could pay you something."

"What's important is that my work here is done. And I'm transferring to you ownership of that DeSoto Airstream to replace your gun-riddled car. Diana and I are returning to Manhattan on the Twentieth Century Limited out of Chicago, the only civilized mode of travel in America."

On the way home, railroad ties furiously clacking under us, I thought about some unfinished business: Nabbing Alvin Karpis and Arthur Barker before the show-off Hoover did. But there was something else that kept nagging at me. What? Was I getting old?

Back in New York, as we enjoyed our buzz from smoking a ritual dual-hose hookah, vanilla-fused shisha loosely packed, Diana and I tangoed to the music of Don Azpiazu and his Havana Casino Orchestra on her Zenith Stratosphere while Kyle coiled in contentment.

Then, disrupting the mellow mood in Diana's penthouse paradise, Walter Winchell's voice burst in, jarring us back to a crude reality.

Good evening, Mr. and Mrs. America and all the ships at sea. Let's go to press. Flash! Mobster Arthur Barker has been pinched by the FBI on a Chicago street. Barker, known as Doc, is the son of the infamous Ma Baker, gunned down in Florida. When arrested, the unarmed Barker said he forgot and left his gun on the bathroom sink. Still on the lam is Public Enemy Numero Uno, Alvin Karpis, Barker's accomplice. C'mon, J. Edgar, when are you going to get serious and nail this fugitive?

At least Karpis—for me—was still in play.

Then I mulled over what had bothered me aboard the Twentieth Century Limited. The matter of the missing Browning that not only launched the War to End All Wars, but eliminated a Cajun State despot.

It must be found and returned to Vienna, its sacred home. Then...

The public is sick and tired of waiting for Alvin Karpis to be captured. This reporter has learned exclusively that a Certain Acquaintance of mine, plans to personally take this violent criminal into custody—no matter the risk to C.A.'s life and limb. God speed, C.A.

...For Jergens Lotion, this is Walter Winchell wishing you lotions of love.

three
Without Fear or Regret 1936

Public Enemy Number One was hiding out in the Crescent City. That's why I was there. To put the cuffs on Alvin Karpis for keeps. And that wasn't the only thing I had to do.

On this expedition I was flying solo, sans Diana, so had my work cut out for me.

A bellhop, boyish and cute, knocked at my suite in the Roosevelt Hotel on Baronne Street, where I was suffering from an incurable hangover from too many Sazeracs—no doubt due to the Angostura bitters. He handed me a letter from Clarence Darrow forwarded from Chicago via New York to New Orleans.

As I tipped the kid, he mentioned suggestively he would be off duty and out of uniform when his shift ended at midnight. I made a mental note.

Darrow's handwriting resembled chicken scratches, but he was an old man, seventy-six, who'd claimed he was through with lawyering—too hoary, too tired, too depleted—so I was surprised to learn he was back at work. The eminent lawyer begged me to go to Chicago to help him on a case.

I wired Darrow I'd be in the City of the Big Shoulders on the Panama Limited as soon as I wrapped up here.

It happened that J. Edgar Hoover was also in NO, staying at the Roosevelt as well, which suggested the Feds were closing in on Karpis—and that Edgar intended to be conspicuously present when it happened. Normally, Hoover's agents would make the bust, but he was smarting under criticism that he wasn't an actual lawman, had no police training, and had never made an arrest, not even for jaywalking.

The schnook wanted to take credit for this apprehension himself.

But not if I beat him to it.

I spotted Hoover and his boyfriend Clyde Tolson in the hotel lobby, but hid behind a palm so they wouldn't see me. I planned to keep it that way.

That said, I wasn't going to allow mere work distract me from the fun and frolic available in this suffocatingly humid, low-lying coastal city, so I occupied a table in the Roosevelt's lobby-level Blue Room to watch the white-tuxedoed Cab Calloway flinging his untamable mop of hair while belting out "Minnie the Moocher":

Hi-de hi-de hi-de-hi / Hi-de hi-de hi-de-hi.

Calloway's band was broadcasting live on WWL, run by Jesuits, whose clear-channel signal reached the nation's nether regions.

At one point, Cab became so ebullient he lost his grip on his baton, which almost smacked me in the eye. I was so taken with his "Reefer Man," "Boog It," and "Peck-a Doodle Doo," I kept the Sazeracs a-coming, wishing Diana was around to prop me up. But job-related issues involving her daytime radio serials kept her and Kyle in Manhattan.

Staggering up to my room after closing down the Blue Room, I found the winsome bellboy of earlier in the day waiting outside my door.

I invited him in, of course, but don't recall much thereafter except that the kid's name was Mickey.

In the morning, the bellboy having decamped, I got a

grip on myself by swallowing a handful of aspirin along with a bucket of java, very black, and returned to business. The first order was to call my message center, Mrs. Prunella Mayhem's Accurate Answering Service ("discreet and confidential"). Mrs. Mayhem's girls always knew what to say and where and how to reach me, something that stymied even J. Edgar Hoover.

My sources were superior to the FBI's, and I'd learned Karpis—born Albin Francis Karpavicius to Lithuanian immigrants in Montreal—was now hiding incognito under the name Edward O'Hara.

There were no messages, so I left the hotel to find an old pal of mine, Papa Celestin, who agreed to drive me around town in his second-hand jalopy, the one he crammed his musicians in during the better days when his Tuxedo Jazz Band toured throughout the South. He was dark skinned and broad featured with a toothy smile, close-cropped hair, always impeccably garbed in a double-breasted.

"Didn't expect you to be back in New Orleans so soon, Tokol."

"Unfinished business, Papa."

A hell of a cornet player, he once recorded for the Okeh label and worked steadily until the Depression swallowed his business and the band scattered. Now he was barely making it as a sometime longshoreman and shipyard welder. On visits to NO when I was a kid—taken there by my dashing uncle who was more of a father than my own—I begged Celestin to teach me the cornet. He did his best, but it was clear I was more suited toward pursuing a something more lucrative than music. Like heisting diamonds.

"Where we all drivin' to, Tokol?"

"Thirty-three-forty-three Canal Street where it intersects

the Jefferson Davis Parkway."

"I know the place. Drugstore on the corner. You need as-pirin or somethin'?"

"I'm about to give someone else a headache, Papa."

When we got to Canal I trained my binoculars on the building across from the pharmacy.

"It's apartment number three I'm interested in."

"Who all's in there?"

"A thug known as Fred Hunter and his hooker-girlfriend Connie Morris. But it's Alvin Karpis I want. He drives there every night for dinner in a Plymouth coupe, plate number one-three-six-two-eight-eight."

We staked out the scene, and as we waited I had this nag-ging, uncertain feeling about The Man With Two Faces. He *was* dead, wasn't he? I saw his body, the staring, lifeless eyes, the foam around his lips, and it was I who shoveled the first scoop of dirt onto both of his faces. Then why did I...

Put it out of your mind, Tokol. You went through a lot with Janus.

After two hours the Plymouth in question pulled up, and the driver got out and entered the building.

"Karpis all right," I said.

"Him? I seen his wanted posters, Tokol, and that man don't look the same."

"He had surgery to alter his appearance. Added lobes to his lobe-less ears. Also an acid bath on his fingers to remove his fingerprints. But, see, he's still got this mortician-like smile. That's why his accomplices call him Creepy."

"You gettin' the cops in on this, Tokol?"

"This one I'm handling myself."

Unobtrusively, I huddled in an adjoining doorway for an-other hour waiting for Karpis to emerge. He finally appeared, a toothpick between his teeth, and walked to his coupe. I was instantly behind him, pressing my Smith and Wesson M&P .38 Special against the back of his neck.

The pinch was a cinch.

"Hands up, Creepy. You make a move my bullet enters your brain, which on principle isn't a bad thing."

The toothpick fell from his mouth.

"Ya got it wrong, mister. The name's O'Hara."

"And I'm Benito Mussolini. Tough luck about your pal Barker and his ma."

"Never heard of 'em."

"I see you've grown earlobes, Creepy. Looks like your jaw's shifted and your nose is a little different. Understand you've had surgery on your fingers too."

"All right, all right." Karpis shrugged, resigned to reality. "Looks like you fingered me, copper."

"Spare me the copper crap. I'm a simple citizen performing a public service."

"Bounty hunter, huh? So you wanna get famous for takin' me in."

"Just the opposite, douchemonger."

"Say, I think I know you. Didn't we almost meet in St. Paul? Tokol ain't it? That ransom thing when you got the victim back and I got the cash."

A sore point with me. I bopped him gently on the back of his skull.

"Ouch!"

"Just wanted to keep you focused, Creepy. Tell me what happened to that mob doctor of yours, Joseph Moran, the guy who operated on your kisser and digits. The Feds wanna talk to him."

"Beats me. Of course Lake Erie's mighty wide and deep."

Bastard wasn't going to squeal.

"Okay, Creepy, march ahead of me to the pay phone outside that drugstore."

"And if I don't?"

"I'll save the government the cost of putting you on trial."

My .38 trained on him, the horn's earpiece cradled at my ear, I dialed the Roosevelt's switchboard and asked for Hoover's suite.

The man himself answered.

"It's Tokol, Edgar. Hope I didn't interrupt you and Clyde in the middle of an intimate moment. I'm in town."

"Why are you here?"

"I came to give you a little present."

Hoover and Tolson once proposed having a threesome with me, but I didn't lean that way. Besides, all my dresses were at my favorite laundry, Zong Hon Wong's on Amsterdam Avenue.

"What are you talking about?"

"A little item called Alvin Karpis."

"Listen, Tokol, I hired you to help us nab Karpis and Doc Barker in that St. Paul kidnap case, but you screwed it up. Lost the ransom, lost the kidnappers."

"But I saved the victim."

"Nevertheless, we landed Barker ourselves."

"But not Karpis. So now, thanks to me, you're getting him on a silver platter, provided the FBI returns the platter with my usual fee on it."

"You mean—"

"Creepy's all yours, Edgar. From the goodness of my heart. Write down this address..."

Within half an hour three dozen FBI agents led by Mike Litvak converged on Canal Street and took Karpis off my

hands. After St. Paul, Litvak and I had kept up our camara-
derie. Mike was a pea-brain and forgot to bring handcuffs, so
he had to use Karpis's own striped necktie to secure his wrists.

When the scene was declared safe, Edgar appeared, bravely lugging a tommy gun he'd never learned to shoot, to sym-
bolically take Creepy into custody while the photographers
and a Hearst Metrotone News cameraman fired away.

I didn't like Hoover much more than Karpis.

All the while, Papa Celestin had been waiting patiently
in his car.

"Where to next, Tokol?"

"Lakefront Airport. I want to see Karpis off."

On the tarmac, where Karpis was bundled onto a Transcontinental & Western Air charter flight to St. Paul to answer
kidnap charges, Hoover told me, "We would have gotten him
sooner or later, Tokol, but I guess I should thank you anyway."

"Damned white of you, Edgar. Say, throw me a bone from
time to time. Not for the cash. Just want to keep my hand in.
Besides, if I can't piss you off I'm doing something wrong."

Standing behind Hoover, Mike Litvak winked at me. He
wasn't keen on Hoover either.

Back at the hotel, the operator put me through to Diana
in New York.

"Hey, dollface, how'd you like an all expenses paid trip to
Chi-Town?"

"What's there?"

"Clarence Darrow."

"I thought he was dead."

"Not to his friends. Meet me there and we'll crawl the
blues joints to hear Alberta Hunter and Big Bill Broonzy, bill
and coo in a fabulous suite at the Drake Hotel, and dine on
steak Diane and cherries jubilee served by the monkey-suits in

the Royal Pumpus Room."

"You need not ask me twice, Tokee, darling."

To indulge ourselves when so many were destitute, hungry, and sick during our terrible depression preyed on my conscience, yet I justified it by telling myself of the unsung good I always did. Nearly always.

In the morning, Papa Celestin picked me up at the hotel. I had one more matter to dispose of before heading to the Windy City.

"Where we goin' now, Tokol?"

"Daytrip. The Baton Rouge Bureau of the New Orleans *Item-Tribune*."

Diana and I had known the bureau's Helen Grey Gilkison since she graduated from journalism school, and if anyone had a line on the missing Huey Long murder weapon she did. Helen had craved a newspaper career ever since she won a *Times-Picayune* high-school essay contest.

When the Kingfish was assassinated she was at the bloody scene, deputized by East Baton Rouge Coroner Thomas Bird to help him search the dead assassin's pockets. Carl Weiss had a wallet containing six dollars, fountain pen, pocket knife, and an engraved calling card.

Helen said, "I don't know why you're so interested in that .32 Browning, Tokol. I saw it myself. It was right next to the body. Weiss bought it in Belgium when he was studying medicine abroad. We know because when he returned to America he filed a customs declaration claiming the gun had a value of eight dollars."

"The gun he brought through customs wasn't the one that killed Long, Helen. He used a different Browning, and that's the one I want. I read that it was pinched at the scene, so it's got to be somewhere."

She sighed. "Okay, after I got your telegram I made a list of anyone who might have swiped it. Coroner Bird, of course. Also John Fred Odom, the district attorney. Highway Police Chief E.P. Roy. All of Huey's bodyguards: Roden, Messina, Coleman, Bates, Votler, McQuiston. A judge named Fournet, a couple of state representatives, Riddle and Wimberly. So it could have been just about anybody. However…"

"Go on, Helen."

"It was snatched by Brigadier General Louis Guerre, head of the Bureau of Criminal Investigation. He's the one who ordered the corridor cordoned off and the capitol locked down. Guerre wanted the gun as a souvenir."

"How do you know this?"

"He showed it to me at a clambake in his backyard. Guerre also had the cartridge clip, six cartridges, and a fired .32 caliber bullet. Told me he's listing it in his will so his daughter will own it someday. Warned that he'd shoot me dead if I put it in the paper, but he never said I couldn't tell you."

"Where does this Guerre live?"

I took leave of Helen after promising to bring her to New York as my guest to see the year's two biggest Broadway musicals, Rodgers and Hart's *On Your Toes* and Cole Porter's *Red, Hot and Blue*.

A little makeup did tricks. Even Papa Celestin was impressed by my disguise as a Cajun crawdad fisherman.

"You look like you just crawled out of the bayou, Tokol. You got the gumbo, all right."

"Tanks, Papa, jest call me Hippolyte Boudreau."

Celestin dropped me off at Guerre's narrow shotgun house, where he sat on his front porch drinking a bottle of Dixie beer that looked so refreshing I almost regretted taking it away from him and batting him on the side of the head with it. Just to get his attention.

"That hurt, dammit," he yelled.

He might have responded more aggressively, but he saw my itchy finger on the trigger of a Smith and Wesson.

"Don't you know who I *am?*" he said.

"Yeah, you're de plaice officer who done swiped dat gun what killed Huey Long."

"What's it to you?"

Guerre seemed to need a little persuasion, so we went inside to talk things over on a more intimate basis.

"You won't get away with this, you bayou bastard," he said.

"Say, I'm vary tursty, Gen'ral. Mind if I finish yo beer?"

"Go to hell."

That merited one broken finger.

"You just signed your death warrant, swamp rat."

That resulted in another finger.

"Now, Gen'ral, I don't got all day. Need to know where dat doggone Browning is."

"Go fuck yourself."

Which produced a black eye.

It took a bit more friendly persuasion, but Guerre finally agreed to turn the Browning over to me. He should have thanked me on his knees for sparing his shooting hand.

"You crawdad eater, we're gonna search every swamp in Louisiana until we find you."

"Gen'ral as my mama used say, pinch de tail and suck de head."

After securing him with handcuffs to the radiator in his *sale de bain*, I said, "Now you jest stay rat cheer till somebody comes and lets you loose."

Then I hopped into Celestin's car for the return trip to New Orleans

"*Laissez les bon temps rouler*," I told Papa, as I removed my disguise.

Back in the Crescent City, I said *adieu* to Celestin and went out on the town.

Despite the startlingly baroque ironwork of the Vieux Carré's gates and balconies and the syncopated rapture emanating from the open doors of the saloons on swarming Bourbon Street, I sensed a forced gaiety—even as a drunk thrust a beer into my hand saying, "Drink, *mon ami*, the Depression won't last forever."

I cavorted intemperately with members of a female voodoo cult on Chartres Street. A woman calling herself Mambo Miriam stuffed a cheap rag doll in my pocket and demanded a hundred dollars, which I gave her without complaint.

She said, "On this doll you'll place an article of clothing belonging to your most bitter enemy, *mon chéri*, and then you'll inject pins into it giving him—or her—agonizing pain and even death."

"But my most bitter enemy has been erased," I told her, referring to The Man With Two Faces.

"But you'll find another one easy."

God knows Mambo Miriam put the gree gree on me.

The next morning, I wired both Darrow and Diana with my travel itinerary. Then, before heading to Rampart Street to catch the Panama Limited from Union Station to Chicago, I engaged a bonded, international courier to personally return to Vienna's Museum of Military History the 7.65-millimeter Browning that had killed Archduke Ferdinand.

I appreciated Gaetano Gagliano's gift-giving gesture, but sometimes you shouldn't tamper with history.

We may have been in a dire depression, but the Illinois Central's all-steel Panama Limited was about class: upper class. I could have flown to Chicago via Peoria on Chicago & Southern Airlines, but speed didn't compare to a Pullman with private compartments, drawing rooms, bath, barber, valet, and ladies' maids the entire route.

I encountered a casual acquaintance on the train, the elegant, bow-tied crooner Gene Austin, whose Victor recording of "My Blue Heaven" sold a million copies. I met him through Diana after Gene made a guest appearance on comedian Joe Penner's radio show on WABC, Columbia's New York station. For most of the trip Austin and I played gin rummy in the club car while he bragged about his exploits as a young American enlisted man under Pershing fruitlessly searching for Pancho Villa in the state of Chihuahua.

America flashed by: Shreveport, Monroe, Jackson, Memphis, St. Louis, Carbondale.

Inside, I dined and slept in luxury, while outside the landscape was littered with boarded foreclosed homes, junked cars, old tires, abandoned refrigerators, and furtive men walking the rails to nowhere. The nation was full of rot and ruin, and I wondered about the fate of our children, such as some baby born in this year of 1936 at, say, Wesley Memorial Hospital in Wichita, Kansas.

Nine-hundred-twenty-one miles and twenty-three hours after leaving New Orleans, the Panama Limited steamed into Chicago's Central Station on Michigan Avenue along the lakefront.

Clarence Darrow himself was on the platform to greet me. He was tall, rumpled, tie askew, suspenders hitching up his baggy trousers, a forelock of his unruly hair flopping over his brow. While he was more stooped than the last time I saw him, his handshake was firm, and his eyes were clear and alert.

We had met a few years ago when I did some legwork

for him in a racially tinged trial in which a Negro doctor was charged with murder after defending his Detroit home from a white mob. I'll never forget Clarence's closing words to the all-white jury.

I have watched, day after day, these black, tense faces crowding this court. Black faces now looking to you twelve whites, feeling that the hopes and fears of a race are in your keeping.

Darrow said, "I thought Diana would be with you, Tokol."

"She's flying in tonight from New York."

Darrow was America's foremost criminal lawyer. His devastating verbal dissection of William Jennings Bryan in the Tennessee Monkey Trial should have been a fatal blow to mysticism and superstition, but religion was impervious to science and reason, especially where the Bible carried more weight than the *Encyclopedia Britannica*.

We took a cab to his home in an apartment hotel at 1537 East 60th Street across from Jackson Park.

"I've lived in this building for the past quarter century, Tokol, and if I'm fortunate, I'll die here."

I greeted his wife Ruby, who busied herself in the kitchen while Darrow and I retired to his cluttered library, shelves sagging with books.

"I'm old, Tokol, tired. Just yesterday I went to Joliet to urge the State Parole Board to release an elderly black man, a former banker imprisoned for embezzlement. I intended to give up my law practice years ago, but somehow one cause followed another, which leads me to why I asked you here."

He shifted uncomfortably in his easy chair.

"I did something I may now regret. It occurred when I represented a young man on trial for murder, Nick Bilinski, who was certain to be found guilty and sent to the electric chair. However, despite the odds I managed a not-guilty verdict."

"Some of your legal arguments are classics, Clarence, such as the one in the Leopold-Loeb case. So it's no surprise you won."

"But it's how I got Bilinski's acquittal that places me in dire jeopardy. It was a controversial case. Nick was a local union leader arrested for killing two men during a bitter coal miners' strike in southern Illinois.

"The lower part of the state is nearly as rich in coal as West Virginia. One of the largest mines is owned by the Chlorite County Colliery Corporation, an obvious target for the Progressive Miners of America. The strike against CCCC was marred by bombings, shootings, and rampages in which the Illinois National Guard was sent to protect the miners brought in by the company to replace the strikers."

"Scabs."

"In labor disputes, the government invariably takes the side of the corporations, so the unions fight back any way they can. When Bilinski, a miner himself, was charged with murder, the PMA hired me as his attorney. He was accused of setting off an explosion that not only killed two strikebreakers but so badly damaged the mine it has shut down completely.

"I talked to Nick at length. God knows he had little—other than his union, a pile of debts, and a wife and four children to feed. And while he was unable to account for his whereabouts on the night of the explosion, I believed with all my heart Nick was not guilty. But the prosecutor, a man named Blaggot, intimidated witnesses, doctored evidence, and seated jurors predisposed against the union.

"It became clear that Nick stood no chance of being acquitted, and the judge, the prosecutor's fellow golfer, was known to be an enthusiastic purveyor of the electric chair. All the eloquence I might muster would never save Nick. So I did the only thing I could do."

He paused for effect, much as he had done in innumerable courtrooms.

"I bought the jury."

"You *what?*"

"Tokol, jury tampering was the only way I could keep a decent, innocent family man from execution due to the prosecution's deceitful case against him. Nick walked out of the courtroom a free man. But he never got his job back and he's still deeply in debt."

For a moment I was at a loss.

"The ethics may not be what one would expect of you, Clarence. But you won an acquittal for an innocent man, so in the long run I don't see the issue."

"Unluckily, my tactics were compromised. Unless I pay one-hundred-thousand dollars, an ungodly sum that I do not have, I'll not only face disbarment and an unfortunate end to a long career, but bribery and conspiracy, which, if proved in court, will mean time in the penitentiary."

"Blackmail."

"Tokol, you were too young at the time so you won't recall this, but in nineteen-twelve I was accused of bribing jurors in connection with a fatal bombing at the *Los Angeles Times* building. While the two defendants eventually pled guilty, I was put on trial. It was never about actual bribery, but solely because I was a defender of the poor, a friend of the oppressed, and a steadfast supporter of labor. Although the jury exonerated me, I cannot face the prospect of a similar ordeal."

"Give me my marching orders, Clarence."

"Reason with this blackmailer's intermediary. At the least lower the amount of the extortion. The go-between calls himself Kana Kealoha."

"What kind of name is Kealoha?"

"Hawaiian perhaps? Kealoha wants cash only, delivered to him personally in Chlorite County, where Nick's trial took place."

"What's the evidence he's using against you."

"I've only seen photostats, but it includes letters with my signature, bank statements, deposit slips, photographs, and affidavits by some of the jurors themselves. I'm not certain how those records fell into the wrong hands. Kealoha claims the documents will be turned over to me once the money has been paid."

That night, I discussed Darrow's dilemma with Diana after she flew in via American Airlines to the unglamorously named Municipal Airport eight miles from the Loop.

"Those long layovers in Buffalo and Detroit almost did me in, Tokee, darling."

She'd been taking flying lessons from Beryl Markham, the first woman aviator to fly solo across the Atlantic from east to west. But Diana didn't yet have her pilot's license.

The Drake Hotel anchored the east end of Chi-Town's North Michigan Avenue. Our tenth-floor suite overlooked the lake, seeming as wide as the Atlantic.

"If we can reduce the extortion amount with this Kealoha character's middleman," I said, "I might pay it myself, but I'm not sure Darrow would go along."

"It's a terrible idea, Tokee, darling. Not only does it capitulate to a criminal, which isn't like you, there's no way to know if this would be the end of it. The blackmailer could possess duplicate copies, additional evidence, and make more demands. Besides, you like a good challenge."

"I'll drink to that."

We clinked our glasses of Camul Veneto Rosso.

I said, "Tomorrow, dollface, we'll drive to Chlorite County, which I understand is the garden spot of the Prairie State."

I bought an inexpensive Packard One Twenty LeBaron Convertible Victoria. It was flaming red with an ox-yoke grill and hexagons on the hubcaps.

"A bit flashy don't you think?" Diana said.

"I want 'em to see us coming. And remember us when we've left."

Darrow had arranged for us to stay in Chlorite City with an old acquaintance of his, Mrs. Maude Wilkens, who owned a guest house.

Out of Chicago we took Route 66 through Joliet, Bloomington, and Springfield. We saw auto camps, motor courts, tourist cabins, roadhouses, and filling stations. Cafes hawking souvenirs, candy, and cigarettes. Diners fashioned like Pullman cars, shacks advertising root beer and famous frankfurters. The telephone-pole monotony was occasionally broken by the small white-on-red Burma-Shave signs…

To get / Away from / Hairy apes /
Ladies jump / From fire escapes /
Burma-Shave

…and the occasional carnival accentuated by cotton candy, Ferris wheel, and tented freak show.

America the ugly.

At East St. Louis, we veered south onto Route 3. From profane Chicago we entered pious evangelical country, passing pretty steepled churches, occasional revival tents, and mourners praying for dead souls in marble orchards. It was farmland with fields of cornstalks rising on either side of the highway, cavernous barns exhorting Red Man chewing tobacco, and ramshackle crossroad burgs in the shadow of elephantine grain elevators.

As we entered Chlorite City, we passed the Miner's Hat Diner with its roof shaped like a coal cracker's helmet, complete with oversized ersatz lamp. It was closed tight, the windows boarded.

"I wonder what the specialty of the house was at the Miner's Hat Diner," I said to Diana.

"Blackened lung, of course, Tokee, darling."

Why Chlorite still called itself a city, I didn't know. Half of the storefronts were boarded up and most of the houses looked vacant, although the hotel was open. What the Depression hadn't taken, the explosion at the mine did.

Maude Wilkens was a sprightly widow who had known Darrow during his apprentice years in Ashtabula, Ohio.

"Clarence was such a dear," Mrs. Wilkens told us. "And so handsome."

We left our bags in her parlor, then sought out Nick Bilinski.

"The CCCC mine is completely down," he told Diana and me as we sat on the decaying porch of his modest frame house. "So I ain't workin'. Sent the wife and kids to stay with her folks in Carbondale. Even though Clarence got me off that murder rap, the union don't have nothin' to do with me no more. If it wasn't for Clarence I'd either be in Stateville or because of the 'lectric chair, six-feet under. I love the man, like he was my own pop."

"Nick, Clarence sent us here to talk to a Kana Kealoha," I said. "Know anything about him?"

"I heard about a stranger in town with some name no one around here can pronounce. Stayin' at the Chlorite Hotel. From what I hear he's a Duncan yo-yo man. Why do you want to talk to him?"

"Clarence has taken a sudden interest in yo-yos."

That night, after a belt-breaking home-cooked meal whipped up by Mrs. Wilkens—far better than Sardi's on West 44th and a lot cheaper—Diana and I compared notes.

I said, "So what's a yo-yo man doing in this godforsaken place?"

"He's stringing us along, Tokee, darling."

"Guy shouldn't be hard to find in a burg this small."

The next morning we encountered Kealoha on the playground of the Chlorite Primary School where he was entertaining the kids with the Elevator, Walk the Dog, Around the Corner, the Creeper, the Zipper, and Skin the Gerbil.

"So you're from Darrow, huh?" he said to us as he packed up his yo-yos and put them in the trunk of his coupe. "You got the hundred-thousand grand? Bills only."

"It'll take a few days to put the money together. Who's your client anyway?"

"You got a lot of moxie, mister. I may be a yo-yo man, but I ain't stupid enough to tell you."

"What's to stop me from turning you over to the coppers, Kealoha, or whatever your name is?"

"Then my client hands the goods on Darrow to the law *and* the Chicago papers, so I ain't worried. The documents is in a safe place. And them shekels better be forthcoming."

"You're actually Hawaiian?"

"Hawaiians is expert in the yo-yo arts."

"There are no Hawaiians in southern Illinois."

"With one exception, and you're lookin' at him."

"The yo-yo's your cover, such as it is. I saw your car on the street. Missouri plates. From St. Louis, I'll bet. I think you're some ex-cop gone bad."

"Back to business, Mr...."

"Tokoloshe. Don't ask. It's from the Zulu."

"You got a counter offer, Mr. Tokoloshe?"

"Fifty grand. Provided I authenticate your so-called evidence first."

"I can tell you right now my client ain't gonna go for it. But I'll let you know. Ya better come up with the dough by the end of the week, and you know where to find me."

Kealoha climbed into his coupe and roared off.

Diana said, "Tokee, darling, we may be better off trying to find the actual blackmailer instead of dealing with this yo-yo individual."

Darrow had given us a list of the principals in Nick Bilinski's murder proceedings, and the one who stuck out was the former state's attorney, George Blaggot, retired after losing re-election, due in part to his blowing the Bilinski trial.

"This Blaggot is the likely suspect," I said to Diana. "God knows he was the closest to the case."

"But, Tokee, if Blaggot had all that incriminating evidence against Darrow, why didn't he use it at the trial? He could have destroyed the accused and his lawyer all at once."

"Greed. It was more profitable to extort Darrow than to accuse him."

Blaggot was now a one-man practitioner working out of his house, where, we understood from Mrs. Wilkens, most of his meager income came from being a notary. The yard was uncut, the front screen door half off its hinges. When we walked in Blaggot was slouched bleary-eyed next to an empty bottle of rye at his desk.

He roused himself when he saw us, and when we explained that we wanted information about the Nick Bilinski trial, he sobered quickly.

"Whad'ya want to know?" he said defiantly. "I prosecuted

that trial fair and square, and all I got for it was getting kicked out of office."

"Clarence Darrow thinks otherwise, that you tried to rig the trial by intimidating witnesses and trying to influence the jurors."

"That's a crock. It was the other way around. If I'd done what Darrow said, how come he won and I lost?"

"Mr. Blaggot, did any of your evidence pertaining to Darrow go missing?"

"What are you saying?"

"It's likely some incriminating material fell into the wrong hands."

"Listen, mister, anything I had is all accounted for, and is boxed in the basement of the Chlorite County Courthouse."

"In my opinion, you withheld a lot of that evidence during the trial and kept it for your own devious purposes."

"The jury heard all there was."

"You're a bitter, defeated man, Blaggot, who is now trying to extort Clarence Darrow."

Blaggot pushed back in his chair, fumbled at a desk drawer, and pulled out a .44.

"I oughta blow your head off, and yours too, lady. Darrow's a dirty word in this house. Now back out of here before I plug you both for trespassing. I'll give you to three. One…"

We did it in two.

Back in the car, Diana, said, "Tokee, darling, that man might have killed us."

"Yeah, but that's not the important thing. He's convinced me he *is* the actual blackmailer. You saw how he hates Darrow."

"What's the plan?"

"Kealoha. Obviously, we're not going to be able to talk to

Blaggot himself again, so now we're forced to go through the yo-yo guy. Of course, we *could* dispose of Blaggot directly."

"You mean…?"

"You brought your blowgun, didn't you?"

"But we have no actual proof."

"Here's how we're going to get it. We shadow Kealoha until he leads us to the blackmailer. Which means, eventually, he'll take us back to Blaggot. As soon as we find the two together that'll cinch it. Case closed."

"We stand out in this place, Tokee, darling. That blazing red Packard One Twenty LeBaron Convertible Victoria you insisted on buying…"

"Naw, we're gonna fit right in."

Diana and I disguised ourselves, she as a farmer's wife in a wide-brim straw hat, striped dress to her ankles, white apron, and clodhoppers, I as a coal miner in helmet and blackened face, carrying a pick.

Diana said, "The pick seems a little obvious, darling. Why are you carrying it?"

"Professional pool sharks pack their own cue sticks, don't they? Why wouldn't miners carry their own picks?"

"You might want to wipe some of that coal dust off your face too."

Diana made me stash the pick in the trunk of our Packard, which was parked ostentatiously in front of Mrs. Wilkens' guest house to throw off snoopers as to where we actually were. We borrowed her battered '25 Ford clunker parked in her garage.

Kealoha appeared none the wiser as we trailed him over the next three days—undoubtedly marking time while waiting for us to come up with the hush money. He seemed to know his way around, sleeping at the Chlorite Hotel, eating at one café or another, driving around aimlessly, doing a little fishing at the pond just outside of town, and seeing a movie called *The Devil-Doll* with Lionel Barrymore and Maureen O'Sullivan at the town's lone theater, open only on Friday and Saturday nights. The movie's title brought to mind the voodoo doll I acquired in the French Quarter, but hadn't used on my new worst enemy. Yet.

Trailing Kealoha was boring—until he finally led us to…

Not Blaggot, but *Bilinski*. Or at least to Nick's house.

"It's not possible," Diana gasped. "Clarence saved Nick from the electric chair."

"Wait a minute. He's not stopping at Nick's."

"Do you think he placed us?"

"Naw, he wouldn't know us by our disguises and the jalopy we're driving. Let's stay on his tail."

Kealoha drove past Nick's, then along a meandering road until he reached the bombed-out mine owned by the Chlorite County Colliery Corporation. After unlocking the gate, Kealoha steered his car into the yard and parked.

"He left the gate open," Diana said. "Probably doesn't plan to stay long."

"Won't hurt to poke around inside."

We hid the clunker in a grove of trees and walked cautiously through the gate. What was left of the mine's auxiliary buildings was either wrecked or boarded up.

"Say, I see the mine's entrance," I said. "If it was sealed, it's open now."

"Let's go in. At least for a minute."

We pushed aside the remnants of a barrier at the mine's mouth and entered. It was dark inside as expected, but we saw, much deeper within the narrow passage, a far-off light, almost beckoning. After walking three-hundred feet or more, we suddenly heard from behind us a rumble, then a boom, and were jolted by the percussive impact of an explosion. We fell to our knees, covering our mouths as the tunnel filled with smoke and powder.

A blast had sealed off the entrance to the mine, with us inside. Even by the meager light of Diana's Zippo, which always accompanied her pack of Viceroys, we determined that the rubble was thick, heavy, and hard-packed. Without proper tools we'd never dig our way out.

"Dammit, dollface, if you'd only let me carry that miner's pick like I wanted to…"

"Shut the fuck up, darling."

Gasping from the dust, we made our way to the light at the far end of the passage. It turned out to be a miner's torch propped on the ground. We were inside a substantial, rock-ribbed chamber, its ceiling far above our reach.

"We're idiots," I said. "Kealoha lured us into the mine, dynamited the entrance, and trapped us."

"We got suckered, Tokee."

"Bastard must have known we were tailing him."

"I told you our disguises were crap."

A slot in the ceiling opened abruptly, allowing in a shaft of light.

Kana Kealoha stuck his head through the opening.

"You folks fine and dandy down there?"

"Kealoha, you bastard," I said. "Get us out of here."

"That's hilarious, Tokoloshe. Tell me another. You think we weren't on to you?"

"We? So Blaggot's in on it with you?"

"Y'know, Darrow's crafty. We figured he'd send some heavies like you and the dame to try and throw a kink in the works."

"Diana," I whispered. "You still have that portable blow-gun of yours?"

"Of course. Stored disassembled in an elegant satin-lined case originally designed for a flute."

"Shaddup, down there," Kealoha yelled. "Where's the dough? You got it?"

"Sure, I've got it."

"Tell me where it is and I'll let you out."

"Not on your phony Hawaiian ass."

"It's gotta be in either that beat up Ford you've been driving or the Packard One Twenty LeBaron. Or maybe in your room at the old biddy's house."

"Or in some hollow stump in the woods. Could be anywhere."

"Listen, Tokoloshe, if I don't find the bills you'll see me just one more time, which will be the last time you'll see anyone but Miss Bitch down there. And even that won't be for long."

"You can't intimidate us, Kealoha."

"No? The mine's doubly sealed off now, and will probably never open again. It's unlikely your bodies will ever be found, so you're standing in your own tomb. What's more, Darrow will be exposed for the fraud he is, his great reputation as a do-gooder shot to shit."

"Quickly," I hissed to Diana. Get that damned dart off *now*."

"I'm trying, I'm trying. I've got to poison the tip. It's dark down here, and I can't afford to slip."

Kealoha said, "The only way out is through this sliding door into an upper tunnel, too high to reach, unless you have a ladder like I got up here, which won't do you no good. Ain't that a laugh? I know this entire mine, a natural cave and all the tunnels dug around it. I was a devil-driver, used to work with Nick Bilinski."

"Bilinski?"

"I worked with a lot of guys."

"You'd leave us here to starve to death?"

"Naw, Tokoloshe, I ain't that kind of guy. Some of the hydraulics in the mine still work, so unless I get what I want, I'll pump out all the oxygen in the room. It'll be quicker for you to go that way. But don't bother to thank me. I'll be back."

"Shoot it, dammit," I muttered to Diana.

Too late.

Kealoha banged the lid shut, and we were again in near darkness, save for the narrow arc of the miner's torch, already flickering, the batteries weak.

"What do you think?" I asked Diana.

"I think he intimidated us."

"Just don't panic dollface."

"Why not?"

"If there's any panicking to be done I'll do it. Now let's see what's in this room while we still have some light."

We found several closed boxes, broken tools, and assorted debris. When we opened the cartons we saw inside hundreds and hundreds of... yo-yos!

I said, "Kealoha must have been using this place as a storage area for his yo-yo scam."

"Okay, Tokee, what's next?"

I paced for a few moments in thought.

"That sliding door up there at the top," I said. "It has a knob on it, so it must have been a regular door once with knobs on either side. Now it just covers the hole."

"So? It's thirty feet up."

"We've got hundreds and hundreds of yo-yos."

"And?"

"What if we were to string a batch of yo-yos together? Make a lasso. Then throw it until it loops onto the knob. We pull on the knob to slide the door so it no longer covers the hole. After that, we use the yo-yo strings as a climbing rope. And each yo-yo serves as a foothold."

"Darling, that's the most ridiculous idea I've ever heard. It's sheer idiocy. Let's start stringing."

We went at it for several hours, mostly in blackness in order to preserve the batteries in the torch. Occasionally, Diana fired up her Zippo so we could confirm our efforts.

Then the ceiling door was pushed aside, and we again saw Kealoha's silhouette filling the opening. He called down to us.

"Tokoloshe, we searched and searched, even had to take down the old bat while we pawed through her house. They took her to the hospital, but don't know if she's gonna make it. We found diddly. Then it occurred to me. There ain't no blackmail money. You never got it together. You and your stacked lady friend drove all the way down here to the land of coal and God, which are one in the same, intending to do us in. You tried to scam the scammers."

"We've got nothing to say to you, Kealoha."

"I got something to say to you, wiseacre. No money, no air. Aloha!"

He slammed the portal shut. Within minutes we heard the sound of a generator starting up, and almost immediately felt the air—that requisite combination of oxygen and nitrogen—subtly, almost imperceptibly, abandoning our awful space, which was now suitable only as a catacomb. About that Kealoha was right.

Diana grabbed my arm. "Tokee..."

"It may take only an hour or two before the pump sucks

out all the oxygen, so let's work fast on those yo-yos. And don't turn on the torch. We've got to conserve the light."

It was a slow, tedious effort braiding the yo-yo strings into multiple strands strong enough to carry our weight, as well as securing the actual yo-yos as footholds.

I felt my lungs depleting, Diana did as well. Existence was running out for us.

"Just don't move," I told her. "Or save oxygen by not breathing."

"You first, Tokee."

Briefly, it occurred to me that our mutual energies might be better put to use by a final, spasmodic carnal diversion—but reality, you bastard you, intruded.

At last our lasso was ready. Then came the tricky part: throwing it high enough to reach and catch the knob. I missed on the first attempt, then the second, third, fourth, fifth.

"Try harder, Tokee, we're almost out of air—and light."

"Doin' my best, dollface."

Again and again and again.

Then, bingo!

"Okay, it's hooked. Now I'm pulling it open."

"Careful, Tokee, not too fast…"

There was always the chance Kealoha had bolted the lid from the top or placed a heavy object on it or even for the door to hit some sort of snag, but… No. Slowly, laboriously, I pulled. The door grudgingly moved, exposing the opening. Within a minute I felt the breath of decent, unused air. Not a rush, but subtle enough to let us know we would make it—provided we could yo-yo our way up to the top.

"You weigh less than me," I told Diana. "You want to claim the honors, climb up there, and grab that ladder?"

"I don't know. Tokee. I'm not very good at heights."

"Aren't you taking flying lessons?"

She managed.

After Diana lowered the ladder to me we were home free. Almost.

When we burst in on Kealoha and Bilinski at Nick's house, the startled Kealoha tried to attack us with a yo-yo, but Diana quickly subdued him with a prick from her blowgun, the dart's tip anointed with a diluted dose of Kyle's venom.

Nick, on the other hand, was remorseful and burst into tears, disposed to spilling his guts.

"Okay, okay, it was Kealoha's idea but I went along with it," he sobbed. "And, yeah, I killed them two scabs. But if I confessed at the time I'd either get life or lit up in the chair. It was an accident."

"No, you bastard, you planted dynamite."

"The surface magazine was where the explosives, detonators, and blasting powder was kept. I knew the layout better than my wife's butt, so I sneaked past the guards. I thought blowin' up the magazine would make a damned pretty show, only I didn't know two union busters would happen along and get in the way. Never meant to kill 'em. But we was on strike, so it was the workers against the owners, and the bosses held all the cards."

"Darrow believed in you, Bilinski. He was sure you were innocent despite Blaggot's criminal case against you."

"Blaggot spooked the witnesses, falsified evidence. Yeah, Darrow got me off in spite of Blaggot, and yeah I conned my own lawyer. So what? He wasn't exactly on the up and up himself."

"He went out on a limb to save you, paying off the jury and witnesses. You knew that and blackmailed him."

"I was desperate. Besides, Kealoha sucked me into it."

"How?"

"We was pals. I knew him from the mines before he went off to St. Louis and learned yo-yoing."

"A Hawaiian in the mines?"

"He only looks Hawaiian. He's Albanian."

"So you and Kealoha, or whatever his real name is…"

"Shkelyim."

"…hatched a plot to extort the very man who believed in you."

"Darrow came out smellin' like a rose, and I got nothing."

"You can't call a not-guilty verdict nothing. He saved your life, Bilinski, and you deceived him. How'd you get all those compromising documents in the first place?"

"The old boy trusted me, confided in me. He roomed in my house, so I intercepted his mail, pilfered his files. He never knew."

"Gimme all the goods you stole from Darrow. Every damned scrap of paper."

"And if I don't?"

"Diana here will kill you."

"Tokee, darling…"

"Or I will."

We decided not to deliver Bilinski's cache to Darrow. He'd be forever haunted for what he did with or without it. So we burned it in the empty parking lot of the abandoned Miner's Hat Diner.

Back in Chicago, when we told Darrow about foiling Nick's blackmail plot, he was both relieved and saddened.

"I trusted that boy. I do not defend his acts, causing the explosion and later trying to extort me, but I understand it. Poverty and desperation drive men and women to extremes beyond their control. You didn't hurt him, did you?"

"He's fine, but the yo-yo guy, who turned out to be an Albanian named Shkelyim, if I'm pronouncing it right, got an adulterated dose of cobra venom. After he came to we took him somewhere where he could contemplate his crimes. The bottom of an abandoned CCCC mine shaft. As for poor Mrs. Wilkens, she was clobbered on the head, but is recovering. Clarence, Bilinski admitted setting the explosion that killed those two men, so shouldn't he stand trial again? He needs to be punished."

"Nick can't be tried again because of double jeopardy. In any event, punishment inflicted for the purpose of giving pain is cruelty and vengeance, and nothing more.

"I wish I had your idealism, Clarence." I sighed in admiration. "Now that the extortion is out of the way, I guess you're ready for your next cause."

"There won't be one. I'm through. I'm spending my days reading the voluminous number of letters addressed to me, some begging me to take on all sorts of cases, most forlorn, foolish, and impossible; many letters asking for money; but most from people anxious to save my soul, and who believe it's their duty to act for God in rescuing me from my impending doom.

"When I was a boy I wondered what the old could find to make it worthwhile to stay alive. Now I know. After you and Diana depart, Mrs. Darrow will fold back my bed and prop the pillows with tender care, and I shall grow deliciously drowsy over the pages of a book, and then drift off into dreams without fear or regret."

Diana and I played tourists for the next three days, after which I donated the Packard One Twenty LeBaron Convertible Victoria to a destitute family on the South Side. I was tempted to again return to Manhattan on the Twentieth Century Limited, but this time we flew because I wanted to waste no time drifting off into dreams without fear or regret.

Back in Diana's Park Avenue penthouse, as we were disrobing in preparation for some romantic coupling, I felt a lump in my coat pocket. It was the rag voodoo doll I'd bought from Mambo Miriam on Chartres Street in New Orleans. I was about to feed it to Kyle, when I decided I might find some use for it after all. You never know. After all, enemies are a dime a dozen.

The Château Cheval Blanc red Bordeaux was dry, but sweet was the silky baritone of Conrad Thibault singing "The Day You Came Along" on the Zenith Stratosphere—until the mood was broken by a familiar, grating voice.

Good evening, Mr. and Mrs. America and all the ships at sea. Let's go to press. Flash! A new poll by the Literary Digest *predicts Alf Landon, governor of Kansas, would whip President Roosevelt with fifty-seven percent of the vote if the election were held today. Your humble scribe takes no sides, of course, but if I had Aladdin's lamp, I'd fix it so that FDR never caught a cold.*

Flash! It seems like only yesterday that my critics blasted me because I reported on divorces and births, and stories like the cross-eyed man whose eyes uncrossed after he was hit by a bus. Now, it's usually some crank who thinks I've insulted Franco, Hitler, Mussolini, Roosevelt, Landon, or someone else. I'm not a Communist, nor am I a Fascist, I'm an American. There's no room for any ism—except patriotism.

Flash! Your obedient servant is about to entrain to Holly-wood to appear in his first starring movie, Wake Up and Sing, *a musical with Ben Bernie, Eddie Cantor, and Alice Fay.*

Flash! Now a W.W. exclusive. This reporter has learned that the NYPD is covering up a violent tong war in the streets of Chinatown, and that the police brass are refusing to acknowl-

edge it. With the cops sitting on their batons, there's only one man equipped to end this bloodshed. My own Certain Acquaintance, who works relentlessly to fight evil and bring criminals to justice. Sic 'em, C.A., but don't get yourself killed.

...For Jergens Lotion, this is Walter Winchell wishing you lotions of love.

four

Tong Wars 1937

The tong wars returned to Chinatown the year FDR was sworn in for his second term—not to say there was any coincidence.

I learned about the tongs from my hip pal Harry Wong who had sweated in his father's hand-laundry during the day while hitting the books at Brooklyn Law at night. Harry, asking for my help, recently hung his shingle on Doyers Street, and was waiting for clients to flock to his storefront. And waiting.

As we sat in my favorite dim sum joint, Woo Fat's on Pell Street, Harry said to me, "Tongs prefer using hatchets and cleavers, Tokol, so their victims are always left a bloody mess."

Harry's father, Zong Hon Wong, operated his laundry on Amsterdam Avenue on the Upper West Side, near the Y where I caught Zs when not crashing at Diana's penthouse. Thus, I got to know and like the Wongs, who put just the right amount of starch in my shirts.

Harry said, "The last tong war was in nineteen thirty-three, Tokol, and it's started all over again. The cops aren't doing diddly. They even deny there's a war."

"I spent some time in the Orient and speak a little of the lingo, Harry, but tell me more about this tong business."

"Mandarin versus Cantonese. Most of the Cantonese in America hail from China's southern mainland and Hong Kong. But there's been an influx of Mandarins from the north and Taiwan, including some young hatchetmen involved in the protection racket—or worse. And they're not limited to Chinatown. Like, they busted the windows of Pop's laundry uptown."

"Maybe they got the wrong Wong."

"Naw, they'd already threatened Pop if he didn't fork up the dough for insurance, so called. Naturally, the Cantonese have organized to defend themselves, but there've been beatings and sabotage—just an overture to the impending carnage. The tongs are brutal."

"Dealing with a tong war may be slightly above my pay grade, Harry. Not sure I know how to handle it."

"Look beyond Chinatown's chop suey joints. These Mandarin interlopers call themselves the Chinese Celestial Benevolent Security and Safety League. Get enough evidence to send 'em to the Big House. Isn't that's what Tokoloshe and Son Cleansing Services is all about? I'm helpless, Tokol. The ink on my diploma's still wet."

The surly server rolled a fresh tray of *har gau*, *jiu cai bau*, *wu gok*, *pei gun*, and *funk zao* to our table, and whatever they were Harry and I made short work of them.

"Harry, I bumped into Captain Moishe O'Hara of the Fifth Precinct at the Policeman's Ball. I hear he's a no-nonsense cop. Don't know him well, but it's said he runs a tight ship."

"Talk him up. I can give you the names of all the Mandarin gangsters. Their top dog's called Fang Chen."

"Address?"

"Eighty-four and one-half Mott Street. It's really a cover for an opium and gambling den that caters not only to Asians but a select number of Caucasians who pay gobs of cash."

"I'll do what I can, Harry, but it'll have to wait until after we fly back from California. Diana and I are going to pay our respects to my pal Ira Gershwin and attend the George Gershwin Memorial Concert at the Hollywood Bowl."

I had been shocked to learn of George's premature death earlier in the year after all the parties I'd gone to at the brothers' Riverside Drive penthouse. I hadn't seen the Gershwins since they decamped to Hollywood.

"Hurry back, Tokol. Until then, slip me five."

We shook on it.

I was sorry for leaving Harry to his own devices, but the Gershwin concert was too important for me to pass up. Besides, Diana was itching to try out her new plane on a cross-country flight.

She was now a licensed pilot and owner of a five-seat Fairchild Model 45, powered by a 225 horsepower Jacobs L-4 radial engine, a flight machine I gave her to mark the anniversary of our introduction.

She and I first locked eyes and more in Tangier, where I was on a secret assignment and she had gone to mend a broken heart, which she refused to discuss. That starry North African night, as we puffed the hookah, was enough for us to know we were kindred spirits, particularly after I learned that her weapon of choice was the blowgun.

I liked women with style.

The plane, which she parked in a hangar at Floyd Bennett Field in Marine Park, Brooklyn, was built to her specs at Fairchild's Farmington, Long Island, plant. After a gentle baptism with a vintage bottle of Moet & Chandon, Diana christened the ship *Hot Mama*, and boldly painted the name on the fuselage.

She'd become bosom buddies with Kenyan bush pilot Beryl Markham, who taught her fly in a Gypsy-powered Percival Gull low-wing monoplane. As an aviatrix, Diana refused to be deterred simply because Amelia Earhart had disappeared over the Pacific near Papua, New Guinea, and was presumed dead, nor by last spring's explosion of the *Hindenburg* at Lakehurst Naval Air Station, which killed thirty-six.

She said, a little defensively, "Flight is now a fact of life."

"Or death," I added in an ominous tone.

Diana handled her takeoffs and landings with aplomb, and was trying to teach me to fly, shaky as I was at the controls. Finally, the maze of dials and switches on the instrument panel started to make sense.

"Hey, dollface," I said, "maybe you'll let me take the wheel now that we're in the clouds."

"Stick, darling, it's called a stick."

After studying the latest aeronautical charts, she figured we'd be in Burbank in two days, including refueling stops. We weren't out to set aviation records, and for me the goal was just getting there in one piece. Diana was damned good, but no Eddie Rickenbacker, and this was her first transcontinental jaunt.

The noise from the engines inside the cabin was wellnigh deafening, but she didn't seem to notice.

America was an amazing place from the air, a farrago of plains, cropland, forests, rolling hills, mountains, and sprawling cities, while vast reaches appeared, deceivingly, to be unpopulated.

Yet the vistas became monotonous as we navigated for endless hours over the heartland, so I read the year's best seller *How to Win Friends and Influence People* by Dale Carnegie. What had I learned so far? To be empathetic, respect others' dignity, never overtly try to win arguments, and shoot to kill only as a last resort.

Safely on the ground in California, we engaged a limo

and driver to whisk us to the Chateau Marmont on Sunset Boulevard, where Diana and I enjoyed a quickie in our suite, then off to the Hollywood Bowl to meet backstage with Ira Gershwin.

"I was devastated when I heard about George," I said as I hugged the self-effacing, bespectacled songwriter, who once sent his doorman Frank with a pump-action shotgun to help Diana rescue me from The Man With Two Faces.

"It's been hard for everyone, Tokol. We were working on a musical called *The Goldwyn Follies* when George began suffering from blinding headaches and hallucinations, which turned out to be a brain tumor. They operated at Cedars of Lebanon Hospital, but it was hopeless."

"A damned injustice. George was only thirty-eight. All that potential lost."

"We sent his body back to New York to be buried at Westchester Hills Cemetery in Hastings-on-Hudson. Thirty-five-hundred people jammed into Temple Emanu-El on Fifth Avenue for his funeral. But my brother's finest tribute will be here tonight in Hollywood."

"I'm not exactly sure how the essence of America is defined, Ira, but George pretty much captured it."

"There are nations in Europe that would have flung out a Jew like him, Tokol, but he was welcomed in America, and he repaid it like a dutiful son."

The Hollywood Bowl, carved into a concave hillside, was packed with an audience of twenty-six-thousand as Diana and I took our seats for the memorial concert, broadcast around the globe with Edward G. Robinson leading the eulogies. Otto Klemperer conducted the Los Angeles Philharmonic, Al Jolson sang "Swanee," Gladys Swarthout "The Man I Love," Fred Astaire "They Can't Take That Away From Me," Lily

Pons "Summertime," and Oscar Levant played the first movement of Gershwin's *Concerto in F*. Not surprisingly, the performance ended with *Rhapsody in Blue*.

After the concert, the line of cars on Highland Avenue, which led from the Bowl, was so heavy, our limo was stuck for two hours, which gave me time to think not only the about American condition, but the Fascist-led revolution in Spain now in its second year, the mad ravings of *Führer und Reichskanzler* Adolph Hitler, Mussolini's brutal conquest of Ethiopia, and Japan's ruthless invasion of China. The disparate elements of the world were on a collision course.

Then I heard on the car radio the robust but calming voice of FDR cutting through the chaos as he called for an international quarantine against the epidemic of world lawlessness: "War is a contagion whether it be declared or undeclared."

God knew there was enough lawlessness in Chicago.

We flew out of Burbank Airport with no issues, Diana at the controls, but somewhere over New Mexico we got into trouble. I was half-dozing when I was awakened by a loud thump and felt *Hot Mama* shake violently.

"We hit some birds, Tokee, but we're okay. I think."

One of the crate's propellers began sputtering and came to a halt, except for the casual drifting of its blades.

"We lost an engine," Diana said. "I'll have to set her down. There's a landing strip in San Ysidro."

"Where's San Ysidro?"

"Nowhere, so if we can't reach it we'll dump in the desert. Plenty of that around, although it's pretty rugged. I'm radioing Albuquerque to let them know our position."

No luck. The radio had power but remained mute, almost like an insult.

"I think the antenna was snapped off when the birds hit

us," she said.

Almost as bad, the compass was knocked off its pin, so it was hard getting a precise bearing on our location, especially with the sun directly above.

Then the remaining engine stalled.

"I'm going to put *Hot Mama* down, darling. Brace yourself."

"Any last words?"

"I think I forgot to water my rubber tree plant before we left."

The plane's wreckage, with our bodies in it, might never be found in the desert remoteness. If we did survive, the wasteland and all its infamy might eat us, denuding further our sun-bleached bones, appreciated only by Gila monsters and scorpions.

Then the ground below *Hot Mama* began to spin wildly. Conceptually, I knew it wasn't actually terra firma in a dizzying whirl but the plane itself, and I wanted to shout, Pull up! But somehow my tongue got to be too much of a mouthful. The noise borne of rushing wind replaced the whirr of the now dead engines, therefore even more terrifying.

Ever closer reeled a kaleidoscopic snarl of scorched bedrock, parched plateaus, ravines, gorges, and strange growths that might be rock, flora, or even human. And then, just before I blacked out, the sickening shudder and jolt of metal at odds with the earth.

I must have been thrown clear of *Hot Mama* in the crackup because when I came to, I felt my body crumpled into a ball on the baked desert clay.

"Diana?" I called out.

She was my first thought as I tried to sit up, blinded by the unrelenting sun. As the blur began to leave my eyes, I distinguished a human shape looming over me.

"Diana, is that you?"

The sinister figure leaned in, and I looked into the terrifying eyes of a war-painted ogre with fang-like teeth. I heard ritualized chanting, howls, and shrieks that amplified into a near-deafening roar.

Over it all came the savage scream, "You are on sacred land, white man, and for that and all else you have done you will die."

Damn, as if things weren't bad enough without being reminded of the evils my covetous forebears inflicted on the folks who had first dibs.

Through the contagion of indefinable shapes and unrelenting clamor, I saw that the fiend was holding what appeared to be a knife in either clawed hand. The fang-like face began to dissolve into another specter. Even before it came into full focus I recognized it. The Man With Two Faces. He was about to throw the knives at me that would pierce my body, channeling me to a hell even worse than the present one.

"But you're dead, Janus, you're dead!"

"Think so, Tokol?"

"Tokee, snap out of it."

I was rallied by sharp slaps on my cheeks as the phantasmagoria evaporated. I never cared much for pain. Even the little bondage games Diana enjoyed mostly failed to amuse me—except the one in which she wore a feathery merkin and I a leather codpiece.

"Sit up, Tokee." Diana's voice.

As usual, I obeyed, although dizzy and weak. Diana always knew best.

"Are you okay, darling?"

"Um, I think so. Must be due to those monkey gland injections I had in Paris."

"I was able to pull out of our dive and level off, but you bumped your head when we hard landed."

The face of the savage who'd threatened me with annihilation looked down at me—only he wasn't a wild man, no fangs, no war paint. And unlike Janus he lacked two faces. He was smiling, wearing denim trousers with a turquoise belt buckle, boots, and a straw hat. Nor did he have a knife in each hand, but a rifle slung over his shoulder, which I learned later he carried to shoot rattlesnakes.

I had suffered another of my recurring nightmares about The Man With Two Faces, which seemed to get worse as each year passed by.

Diana said, "We're on the Tamaya Indian Reservation, and this is Bobby Menchego who lives a few miles up the way. He's fluent in Keresan, the original language of the Tamayan people."

"Howdee, bub," Bobby said. "Saw ya'll go down. Good thing I come along in my old pickup. Road's just over yonder. It's dirt but it gets you there."

"I must have hallucinated," I said.

"Desert plays funny tricks sometimes. Say, ya'll might have been stuck out here all night if I ain't come along. Freeze your Eastern asses."

"Bobby's family is part of the Santa Ana Pueblo," Diana said. "They've been working this land since the fifteen-hundreds—before the Spaniards."

I said, "When we went down I was sure we weren't going to make it."

"*Hot Mama*'s a bit banged up, Tokee, but nothing that can't be fixed. Bobby's going to tow her in his pickup to Albuquerque. Find out what went wrong with those engines."

Bobby said, "Ya'll kin stay the night at my place, if you don't mind four kids and five dogs runnin' around like fools. For dinner, the wife's makin' spiced pork, wild sage bread, corn puddin', baked pumpkin, and in the mornin' blue corn flapjacks and ranch eggs."

Bobby Menchego's plain adobe was filled to the timbers with people and pets, including an argumentative chicken, Henrietta, who had the run of the place. The entire family joined in to sing medieval songs of lore strummed on an autoharp by Bobby's wife Sally, such heirlooms as "When the Bloom is on the Sage," "Cool Water," "Tumbling Tumbleweeds," and "It Looks Like Rain in Cherry Blossom Lane."

At chess, Bobby may not have been a Capablanca, but he beat me three out of four games, the fourth being a draw. Sally insisted Diana and I sleep in their bed, while they camped on the floor. The Menchego homestead was noisier than Hollywood's pretentious Chateau Marmont, but a lot more fun and way less expensive.

After driving us to Albuquerque, the Fairchild in tow, Bobby adamantly refused our offers of compensation.

Diana told him, "Here's my address. Bobby, you have a standing invitation to visit us in New York anytime. We'll show you the sights, take you to a Broadway show, escort you to the great museums, and treat you to the Rainbow Room. Our door is always open."

"Thanks, ma'am, but we're not allowed to leave the reservation. That's a joke."

With *Hot Mama* stashed at West Mesa Airport for repairs, Diana and I checked into the Hotel Villa Condesa, tucked away on Romero Street near Old Town Plaza and San Felipe Neri Church. All adobe with beamed ceilings, tile floors, and hammered-tin chandeliers, the hostelry suited our sense of aesthetics, as did the neighboring buildings of stucco, terra-cotta, and wood. The Santa Fe Railroad Station was a quick cab ride away, and, of course, Route 66 would lead us to about anywhere between LA and Chicago.

From the lobby I phoned person-to-person to Harry Wong in Manhattan.

"Tokol, you've gotta come back now."

"Your father?"

"Pop's okay, but he boarded up his laundry and went into hiding. The tong's killed at least five Cantonese, and I found out there've been even more murders no one knows about. The killers are hiding the corpses so few outside of Chinatown are aware of the feud. We're a closed community here."

"Harry, I don't know how long we'll be stuck in Albu-querque. Our plane made an emergency landing, so it's in the shop for a fix."

"Why do *you* have to be there, Tokol? I thought planes were Diana's gig."

Point taken.

She agreed to stay in New Mexico to nurse *Hot Mama* while I caught a commercial flight back. As much as I flew, I was at heart a rail man, adoring the elegance of the Broadway and Twentieth Century limiteds, loving the tactile vibrations under my heels of a Pullman, steel against steel. But Tokolos-he and Son Cleansing Services had disinfecting obligations around the globe, so there were times you just hadda go faster.

Back in New York, it didn't take me long to realize Cap-tain Moishe O'Hara of the Fifth Precinct in Chinatown was a variegated piece of work. His brogue was as thick as his brawn, and he couldn't resist the occasional Yiddish obscenity.

"Sure'n, I remember you from the Policeman's Ball, Mr.

Tokoloshe, and that generous contribution you made to the Patrolmen and Detectives Widows and Orphans Asylum on Staten Island, but I guarantee you there ain't no tong war in Chinatown. They're just rumors. The tong wars is all in the past."

"I understand there have been at least five murders here in your precinct in the past week, maybe more."

"Random violence. Happens every day in a big city. At least we ain't as bad as Chicago."

"But these have all been in Chinatown."

"Pure coincidence."

"Are you familiar with an opium and gambling den on Mott Street, Captain?"

"Street, yes, opium and gambling, no."

"Then how about the Chinese Celestial Benevolent Security and Safety League?"

"A group of outstanding young Asians doing decent work on behalf of their people, and assisting them what recently immigrated to our shores."

"I have some names—"

"Got all the names I need."

"Captain, you don't seem to know much about what's happening in your own precinct."

"And you don't seem to know when to shut your trap. Sergeant, come in here and show this *ku fartzer* to the door."

"You seem a bit sensitive about all this, Captain."

"Tokoloshe, you keep up this crap and you'll find your own corpse in some alley with an axe decoratin' your skull."

"That a threat?"

"A friendly warning, *kafin kup*. For your own good. Chinatown's a different world for foreign devils like you."

"Foreign devil?"

"That's what the Chinese call Caucasians."

"But you're a…"

"I got special dispensation."

It was clear I was going have to deal with the tong war without the help of O'Hara and the Fifth Precinct.

Garbed as a longshoreman, with a patch over one eye, I called on Harry at his Doyers Street law office, empty save for Harry, a second-hand desk, and two flimsy chairs.

"Jeez, Tokol, I didn't recognize you at first," he said.

"I'm disguised because things could go south for you if the tong connects us."

"Did you speak to O'Hara?"

"The man's a pill. Offered me squat. Listen, Harry, I've got to get into that tong headquarters on Mott Street to ask questions. How do I do it without raising suspicions? I can't just knock at the door and be welcomed in."

"Go as some rich, white dude eager to play fan-tan or eat opium. Caucasians are tolerated if they bring enough cash, and I mean a lot. I happen to know that Baldrick Ponsby Smythe, a director of First Guaranty Credit Trust Corporation is a regular. So's Max Ziegfeld, a cousin of the late Broadway impresario. Also the thoroughbred owner Alistaire van der Potts."

"Say, I know Smythe. Bailed him out of a big jam once. He owes me. I think I'll use old Baldy as a referral. Whether he knows it or not."

"It'll be dangerous, Tokol. More than one person has gone inside the building and never come out. It's said the basement's a graveyard. There are even rumors that Ambrose Bierce is buried there."

"I can take care of myself, Harry. Haven't played fan-tan since my days in Singapore. I'm a bit rusty but up for it."

On Mott Street I knocked at the barred door of the Chinese Celestial Benevolent Security and Safety League, identified only by a small, nondescript sign containing Chinese characters, and in a boarded window a placard in English reading STOP JAPANESE AGGRESSION, a sign appearing in every store window in Chinatown.

As I waited, stereotypical images of ancient China flowed through my mind: peasants bending knee-deep in water harvesting rice; teeming, narrow streets swarming with jinrikshas pulled by coolies; silhouetted junks at sunset with their high poops and battened sails; the Great Wall snaking into infinity; fat, grinning, self-satisfied Buddhas; fierce warlords, draped in robes, sitting with legs apart, surrounded by concubines.

Finally, the door opened somewhat wider than a crack and a scowling Asian man peered out.

"What you want?"

"*Nín hao*, as we used to say in Macau. Smythe sent me."

"Who?"

"Baldrick Ponsby Smythe, one of your regulars."

"Who you?"

"They call me Tokol. I'm here for the fan-tan."

Suspicious, the man looked into the street, right, then left. Concluding that I was alone he let me in.

I said, "May I ask your name, sir?"

"Me Fang Chen."

"Do I call you Mr. Chen or Mr. Fang?"

He ignored my question with a snort.

"You give me two thousand up front," he said. "Then you play fan-tan."

"I didn't think to bring that much with me."

"I take check."

Which I wrote on my numbered-only account at Banque

Cantonale de Genève.

Seemingly satisfied, he led me from the outer room to a flight of stairs. I noticed several torpedoes in coolie clothes eyeing me suspiciously, looking for trouble. Although I was packing iron I wasn't sure if I could shoot my way back out to the street, outnumbered as I was. On the second floor we passed a succession of small rooms to a larger one where fan-tan was underway at several tables. The players were mostly silent and intent, the air torpid with cigar smoke and the odor of hops and *baijiu*. A doll-like Asian serving-wench kept the booze flowing.

Fan-tan was a deceptively simple game dating to Chinese antiquity. It involved a banker, a bowl, and a handful of dried beans. Players bet on the number of beans under the bowl while gradually the banker divided the beans as the players gambled on the remainder.

Nobody acknowledged me as I took my seat, but I surreptitiously studied the faces of the players. I recognized one of LaGuardia's deputy mayors, the sanitation commissioner, two state assemblymen, and the pastor of the Seventh Avenue Presbyterian Church.

Fang Chen himself sat in as the banker at my table.

It was only after I began to win that the other players took notice of me, in particular an idiot I knew from the newspaper society sections: Heathcote Whitney Hathaway. He got drunker and more belligerent as his losses mounted. I estimated he was out by thousands.

And that ain't beans.

Millions of Americans were starving, literally, but Hathaway made no concession to the Depression, and was the type to squander a fortune only to forget about it the next day. He was also testimony to the fact that being rich did not make one smart.

Suddenly, he stood, knocking over the table, sending the bowl and beans flying, and pulled a gun from his coat. It was an antique Nepperhan .31 percussion pocket revolver with a blue silver-plated barrel. My beloved weapons purveyor Gaetano Gagliano, had one for sale recently, and likely this was it.

"This game's crooked!" he shouted, voice slurred, as he fired a shot into the pressed-tin ceiling. "I never took a loss like this before, so I know it's fixed."

The players scattered in panic, some ducking under tables, other running for the stairs.

Hathaway yelled at Fang Chen, "Fork over my dough or I'll shoot you in your yellow belly. You're not taking advantage of me just because I'm a Hathaway. It's the principle on account of I could buy every man here in a heartbeat."

As if Hathaway knew something about principles.

Fang Chen kowtowed and handed Hathaway a wad of bills.

He counted the money in satisfaction and then threw it into air, the bills fluttering down, before returning the Nepperhan to his coat pocket.

"Keep your damned dough, rice ball. Last time I'll gamble in this place. I'm siccing the dicks on you. Going to close this join down."

Hathaway may or may not have been right that the game was crooked, but he was unassailably and incontrovertibly correct he would never play at Fang Chen's again.

He did not reach the door.

Fang Chen neatly, and with butcher-like professionalism, split the back of Hathaway's patrician skull in half with a meat cleaver.

The fan-tan players, those left in the room, watched gaping as Fang Chen's minions swiftly scooped up the bills and the revolver, removed the body with the cleaver still protruding from what was once Hathaway's brain, and mopped up the blood. Then the tables were reset and the games continued. Just as silently and intently as before.

Why should a little murder disrupt fan-tan?

I went on to enjoy significant winnings, although I suspect Fang Chen let me score as an incentive to return. As I was leaving I encountered him in the hall.

I said, "Are you aware you just murdered an important New York society figure?"

"Yes."

"Questions will be asked."

"What Mr. Hathaway say about the police not permitted, even though we have arrangement with them."

"What happens when his body's discovered?"

"Will not happen. We have hidden place for it."

"But there were lots of witnesses, including a deputy mayor. Someone will—"

"No one will talk. The secrets of house will remain here, and if anyone, yellow or white, reveals our private matters, he and every member of his family, children to grandparents, will die agonizing death. It is the way of the tong. Did not Mr. Baldrick Ponsby Smythe explain this to you before you came?"

"Not in so many words."

"Then this will put you on notice, Mr. Tokol."

I had a lot to process. Hathaway's murder, names to register, faces to remember, Fang Chen's threat.

As I prepared to go down the stairs, I smelled the mystical fumes of the pipe, familiar to me from my days in the Orient. I followed my nose and entered a long, narrow warren, quite dark, where I saw a series of wooden bunks on which men were reclining. Some were asleep, others on their sides smoking elongated pipes.

Fang Chen approached me from behind.

"You like?"

He held a pipe, needle, lamp, and a jade box carved with images of kewpie doll maidens and fire-breathing dragons, which I knew contained opium.

I recalled from my previous voyages in pipe dreaming, that while smoking, all my ominous and apocalyptic thoughts vanished, and I'd find myself floating as if reaching Valhalla, the true nirvana, not some farfetched theological theory for it. But now I resisted. I wasn't ready to soar to an opiated-engineered heaven, particularly one that required ever increasing return visits.

"Maybe next time, Fang Chen."

"You come back. Me like you. Bring money."

About to depart the opium lair, I observed, apparently comatose on one of the cribs, a bulky gent who appeared familiar. Looking closer I saw he was Police Captain Moishe O'Hara.

Fang Chen ushered me to Mott Street where, after the semi-darkness inside, the afternoon glare blinded me like an explosion of suns.

I relayed my experience at the Chinese Celestial Benevolent Security and Safety League to Harry Wong as I sat on a wobbly chair across from his desk.

He said, "You risked your life, Tokol, but, obviously, not as much as the late Heathcote Whitney Hathaway."

"Fang Chen's isn't the place for a drunken outburst, no matter how rich you are."

"Hathaway's body will never be found. I understand the number of tong murders is escalating, but the police list the victims only as missing persons. Even the press isn't reporting it." He sighed. "Tokol, this has gotten too big for either of us. Maybe it was a mistake involving you."

"No, Harry, the key is getting the fuzz to move. I now have something on Moishe O'Hara that might make him act, whether the prick likes it or not."

Diana returned to New York sooner than expected after solo-flying *Hot Mama*, her engines mended, from Albuquerque.

She said, "It was a failure of the magneto switch, which came loose in flight due to a flawed bolt assembly. Yes, Tokee, darling, a stupid, defective bolt. The malfunction was no doubt made worse by the bird strike."

We celebrated her safe return on brownstone-lined Swing Street, where the jazz joints shouldered both sides from Fifth to Sixth. Leon & Eddie's, the Famous Door, Jimmy Ryan's, the Spotlight Club, and the most celebrated, the Onyx Club at 62 West 52nd.

Without the hearts and souls of black musicians, jazz wouldn't exist, and Swing Street was one of the few fully-integrated places in America. Diana and I were regulars at the Onyx, a one-time speakeasy, where the cigarette smoke was as engulfing as a London fog. Its proprietor, ex-bootlegger Joe Helbock, always gave us a ringside table.

"Tokol, Diana," he said, "you guys ain't been in for awhile."

"We flew cross country, Joe." I said. "Had a little mishap somewhere over New Mexico. But we're back in good form."

"Gotta surprise for you. Guess who's gonna be jamming after hours tonight? Bunny Berigan, Art Tatum, Benny Goodman, Django Reinhardt, Lester Young, and Maxine Sullivan. Ya won't find that lineup in one place again."

Deep into morning, sated and orgasmically fulfilled by the healing genius known as jazz, I laid out for Diana a plan to end Chinatown's tong war.

"It's tricky, Tokee," she said. "Lots could go wrong."

"I need to return to Fang Chen's when Captain O'Hara's in the building. I learned from Harry that O'Hara's always there on Friday afternoons, sometimes doesn't leave for two days."

"I'll go with you."

"Impossible. The only women allowed are Chinese concubines, harlots, and wenches."

"I'm superb at disguises. Have you ever seen me as a gun moll?"

"I have a better idea. Camouflage yourself as Apple Mary selling Granny Smiths, Cortlands, and Winesaps across the street. Use your Graflex Speed Graphic concealed under a babushka. I need photos of anyone entering or leaving, particularly O'Hara."

"And you?"

"I'll be inside with my Minox Riga."

Unlike Diana's weighty Speed Graphic, the favorite of my cigar-chomping press photographer pal Weegee, the Minox Riga was tiny, easy to conceal. Mine was an experimental model personally assembled by its inventor Walter Zapp, a genius I'd met while doing hush-hush work in Tallin, Estonia. Zapp's camera had a 15mm f/3.5 lens using 8x11mm film, but with extraordinary resolution—even in the dark.

Zapp, eyes bulging behind his thick glasses, told me at the time, "I decided cameras were too heavy, so I built one that could fit in the palm of my hand. And you're holding it, Tokol. Just don't get caught."

I knew Zapp's camera would one day become the rage

among spies.

Fang Chen met me when I returned to the Chinese Celestial Benevolent Security and Safety League, extracted an enormous roll of cash from me, and, at my behest, led me to the place of pipe dreams. As expected, Moishe O'Hara was there, serenely smoking, the room otherwise empty. I took the crib next to his.

"Hello, Captain, mind if I join you?"

A mumbled non-response.

Fang Chen assembled all my accoutrements, watching as I fired the lamp, tamped the opium into the pipe's bowl, holding the bowl over the flame, inhaling, allowing the smoke to curl, and experiencing the first sensation of euphoria.

"Ah, you do this before," he said.

"I'm an old China hand."

Soon I heard a ringing in my ears like that of celestial bells. But I warded off the overwhelming compulsion to take another puff. I was on the job.

"I leave now," Fang Chen said. "Go to fan-tan room. You smoke. Enjoy."

"Don't worry about me, Fang Chen," I said raising the pipe to my lips.

After he slipped out, I spoke softly to my somnolent neighbor while he lay on his side in the adjoining bunk.

"You don't remember me, Captain?"

"*Fercockt.*"

Which I happened to know was Yiddish for "all fucked up."

"What would your superiors say if they knew you were an opium eater, a habitué of a notorious gambling den, and a man whose been bought by the tong to hide their war?"

He attempted to sit up, trying to focus through half-lidded

eyes. His voice was slurred.

"You're that Tokoo or somethin'. Some wise guy. You ain't gonna get out of here alive."

"Relax, Captain. Consider me an old buddy. Let's smoke together to share all the joys of the immortal soporific."

"*Gay avek*," he said, telling me in mumbling, nearly incoherent Yiddish to go away.

"Shall I help re-light your dreamstick, Captain?"

Which I was more than delighted to do. O'Hara's eyes glazed over.

With Fang Chen occupied at fan-tan, I took photos of the comatose captain with my Minox Riga from every angle and position, including close ups showing the opium pipe at his lips, the spittle running from his mouth, and his uniform with the badge and its number clearly visible.

Now, I had to get the hell out of there.

I pocketed the camera and put the opium paraphernalia aside, thinking I might slip out unnoticed. But nothing ever happens the way it's supposed to.

"Where you go?"

Shit.

Fang Chen was back, and holding a meat clever at his side.

"I thought you were dealing fan-tan," I said. "Don't let me take you away."

"You not smoking. Why you not smoke?"

"It just it occurred to me I have an appointment uptown on Vanderbilt Avenue with FDR's Treasury Secretary Henry Morgenthau. Hank never makes a move without me. So I'll have to come back later."

"This not right. You gave me much money. No one leaves so soon. Mr. Baldrick Ponsby Smythe is in fan-tan room. He say he know you but never told you about this place."

"Old Baldy's forgetful, that's all. Millionaires are like that. They hire other people to remember things for them."

"You lie. Mr. Smythe never sent you here."

"Maybe I will stay, Fang Chen. Just let me fire up the opium lamp. Ah, yes, there it goes, nice and hot. Very hot."

"No like you no more. I put you away."

He raised the clever, about to bring it down on me the way a butcher separates a pork shoulder. But I was too fast for him. I scooped up the red-hot opium lamp and flung it into his face. My hand was scorched, but not as badly burned as Fang Chen, with the oil-fueled flames blistering his eyes, blinding him, causing him to drop the clever.

He fell to the floor, screaming and writhing in agony, as I ran into the hall and down the stairs to the main floor, shouting, "*Bangzhù! Bangzhù!*" which I understood to be "Help! Help!" in Mandarin.

Instantly I was surrounded by coolie-clad goons.

"Upstairs, quick," I said. "It's Fang Chen. He's been hurt by some sort of explosion. Go, go go."

Upstairs they ran, while I scurried out the front door, absconding into the winding alleys of Chinatown. A close call. But I was conditioned to narrow escapes.

Later, I joined Diana for *ngao yuk kau* and tea at Woo Fat's and described my adventure at the opium den.

"It took all my willpower not to take that second puff of poppy," I told her.

"You've never been a slave to temptation."

"Except for you."

"Don't get schmaltzy on me, Tokee, darling. How's your hand?"

"Smarts, but I'll survive."

"That was so brave of you, picking up a hot lamp burning with oil. Let me kiss your hand for you."

"Save it for tonight, dollface. Golly, I hope Fang Chen wasn't seriously burned."

"You're all heart."

"And what about your day, Apple Mary?"

"I took some superlative photographs of a variety of gangsters and gamblers entering and leaving Fang Chen's, not the least of whom was Captain O'Hara himself. How about you?"

"My own pictures of him couldn't be more compromising."

"I'm sure he'll be delighted to learn about it."

That night we developed our film in Diana's penthouse darkroom, blowing up the photos into quality oversized glossies. I made several sets.

"The next step is yours," I told her. "Best I stay out of the picture, so to speak."

When Diana, togged to the nines, went to the Fifth Precinct stationhouse to talk to O'Hara, she was ushered right in to his office.

She later gave me the low down.

"What can I do for you, miss?" O'Hara asked her.

"It's more about what I can do for you."

"Begorra, this is gettin' interesting. Y'know, you're one hell of a pip, lady. Should I close me office door?"

"It would be wise, Captain."

O'Hara shut the door, then, leering, scooted behind his desk.

"I've something for you," Diana said, as she removed from her purse a large envelope containing the photos, and put it in front of him.

"I like surprises," he said. "French postcards? Heh, heh."

O'Hara opened the envelope and saw himself in all of its unmitigated squalor.

"*Oy gevalt!* Where'd you get these?"

"That's beside the point."

"And you said you came because you could do somethin' for me. Sure'n, it's obvious you're tryin' to bleed me. Listen, sister, I'm gonna burn these photos and put you in handcuffs meself."

"That wouldn't be in your interest, Captain. You see, there's more than one set. Are you familiar with the Beaux Arts clock in the lobby of the Astor Hotel in Times Square?"

"Who ain't? So what?"

"If I'm not there in exactly one hour a friend will dispatch duplicate sets of these photos to all eight daily newspapers, the mayor, police commissioner, governor, attorney general, each state representative from New York City, J. Edgar Hoover—and, most important, Walter Winchell. So don't even think about putting your paws on me."

"If it's long green you want, you damned *nafka*…"

"It's not money. These are your instructions. You're to meet with Harry Wong, a young lawyer who's just opened a practice in Chinatown."

"Ah ha. So it's this ferkin' Wong character who's behind all this."

"Harry knows nothing about the photos—or even that you're directly mixed up with the gangs. But he's an expert on the tongs, and he's fully aware, despite your denials, that a deadly gang war is underway. He wants to end it, that's all.

"So you'll work with Harry in exposing the tong leaders, including Fang Chen and the bogus Chinese Celestial Benevolent Security and Safety League. Your men will raid it, put all inside under arrest, and ensure they're brought to trial, thus bringing the tong war to an immediate close.

"Here's a list of the names of everyone in the Mandarin tong faction, with many accompanying photographs. Oh, and you'll want to dig in the basement of the Chinese Celestial Benevolent Security and Safety League. I think you'll find a lot of important evidence, and perhaps even solve the mystery of a number of disappearances. But don't step on the lime. It's not good for shoe leather. Meanwhile, you may keep all the photos of yourself and the others. There are plenty more. All suitable for framing."

I'd been afraid O'Hara might try to strong-arm her or worse before she could take a powder, but Diana insisted she was prepared, her blowgun-mini primed and ready in her purse for instant defense.

She split from the Fifth Precinct stationhouse unscathed, unruffled, and elegant, as usual.

The tong war came to an abrupt end with a police raid on the Chinese Celestial Benevolent Security and Safety League, scores of arrests, including Fang Chen, and the recovery of more bodies than the public ever dreamed. A few of the society gamblers, such as Baldrick Ponsby Smythe, turned state's witnesses.

Despite the kink in his opium habit, Captain Moishe O'Hara was celebrated as a hero, praised by Winchell, upped to deputy chief, and was grand marshal of both the Jewish Great War Veterans parade, protesting the Nazi persecution of German Jews, and the St. Patrick's Day parade.

Back at her penthouse, as I plotted my next mission, Diana and I toasted with daiquiris, which I learned to mix during my brief period as a rum runner out of Havana, which came to an end only after rival rum runners rammed our boat and sank it.

We were interrupted by her doorman, phoning from the lobby.

"Tokee, darling, you'll never guess who's on the way up."

When she opened her door, in flooded the entire New Mexico Menchego family: kids, dogs, and Henrietta the chicken, who immediately went to investigate Diana's pet king cobra Kyle. Sally's autoharp dangled from a strap over her shoulder.

"Howdy, folks," Bobby said, still wearing his regulation denim, boots, and straw. "We left the reservation. Y'all said your door was always open, so here we are."

Diana said, "Bobby, so unexpected. How did you get here?"

"In the old pickup. Only had two flats. Sure is a lot of buildins' in this burg. Say, which one is that there Rainbow Room you was talkin' about?"

The Menchegos pitched their tent on the living room floor. Being a desert family they were unperturbed about Kyle. We showed them the sights, treated them to *Shall We Dance* with Astaire and Rogers, and introduced them to Winchell at Table 50 at the Stork Club.

Good evening, Mr. and Mrs. America and all the ships at sea. Let's go to press.

Flash! Nazi Germany has become a threat to world peace. It's criminal that a thug like Hitler could rise so high in politics. His hatred of the Israelites is contemptible, and when an assassin shoots him down no sane man will mourn. Meanwhile, to our shame, an isolationist movement is growing in America led by the Lone Ostrich, Charles A. Lindbergh, who is on my drop-dead list. I say to all you Nazi lovers in America, you Razis, your death threats against me won't work. My pal J. Edgar Hoover's got my back.

Flash! This reporter has learned that a Nazi spy ring is operating with impunity under our very noses, and yet the authorities seem to know nothing about it. But one man does: C.A. My Certain Acquaintance is putting his life on the line to bring down this abominable espionage conspiracy, and C.A is well aware of what the Nazis do when they catch an infiltrator in their midst.

...For Jergens Lotion, this is Walter Winchell wishing you lotions of love.

five

Nazis 1938

We weren't at war with the Nazis. So why did Dedrick Leitner try to kill me?

Maybe because I got wind of Leitner's sweet little spy ring? Still…

It all began at a new jazz club called Café Society opened by Barney Josephson, a newcomer to the city, in the basement of 2 Sheridan Square in the Village.

I was fond of the neighborhood, and once crashed at a pad on Carmine Street, sharing a mattress with Gaetano Gagliano, a nearsighted goombah crony caught up in the fracas between Joe The Boss Masseria and Salvatore Maranzano, who declared himself *capo di tutti capi*. That was in 1930, a tale for another time. Gaetano taught me all I knew about firepower.

Despite the hoards of uptown tourists crowding the watering holes and coffee houses in the narrow Village streets, one could live there mud cheap, which is why it drew so many down-and-outers pretending to be writers and artists, such as the poet Max Bodenheim. He wore dark glasses and claimed to be blind as he begged for coins at the edge of Washington Square, and from time to time I stuffed his tin cup.

Even though they hosed down the streets at night it was a dirty place.

You didn't have to dress up to get a table at Café Society, so Diana and I dressed down, she in turban hat, puffed-sleeved shirt, and blue poplin palazzo pants—all of her own design; I in v-neck sweater, high-waisted, heavily-pleated plaids with extra cuffs, and my gat in an ankle holster.

There, the swells weren't treated better than anyone else no matter how much folding green they dished out. The dive appointed a doorman, but was so egalitarian the patrons were required to open and close the doors themselves. It was the first club in New York outside of the jazz joints on West 52nd to dash racial barriers, so the bigots had to get their kicks elsewhere.

Barney was a young guy who rode into town with seven ones and a fifty-cent piece in his pocket—plus the argyles that dressed up a pair of snazzy shoes. His old man being a cobbler, Barney, as a fashion statement, wore patent leather, black-and-white wingtips.

Reared in Jersey, he formerly sold footwear at his family's shop in Trenton. Barney had opening-night heebie-jeebies, so Diana and I sat with him as he confessed knowing more about soles and heels than cabarets.

"It bugged me that the only way blacks could visit a club outside of Harlem was to play in the band," he said. "So I borrowed six grand and opened this joint. I call it a political cabaret with jazz, which is why that effigy of Hitler dangles from the ceiling over the Steinway."

"Nice touch," I said. I was impressed.

Barney billed himself as a saloon impresario.

"I'm not hiring a line of half-naked dancing girls or Negro comics who play on white stereotypes of blacks."

Word got around. The opening night headliners were Billie Holiday and boogie woogie piano hotshot Big Joe Turner, while Jack Gilford, a comedian discovered by Borsch Belt comic Milton Berle, was MC.

The room, exceeding the official seating capacity of two-hundred ten, included Clare Boothe Luce, Tallulah Bankhead, Paul Robeson, and Orson Welles. I also recognized right-wing columnist Westbrook Pegler sitting at a table with a skinny creep who seemed to have shrunk inside his double-breasted worsted.

I loathed the horse-faced Pegler for every incendiary word that spewed from his poisoned pen. I had met the man at some dull society affair Diana dragged me to, and after he uttered ten words I was tempted to floor him. Somehow, however, I managed to appear more or less civil.

Big Joe Turner, a three-hundred pounder, floored us with "Roll 'em Pete," "Low Down Dog," and "It's All Right, Baby," while Billie slithered under our skins with "God Bless the Child," "If Dreams Come True," and "I Can't Get Started."

As we were leaving, we passed Pegler's table, and he grabbed my sleeve, which made me want to shudder.

"Mr. Tokoloshe, do you remember me? We met at a party on Park Avenue. Had a lively chat, as I recall."

"How could I forget, Pegler? We discussed that new term you coined in the *World-Telegram*, bleeding hearts, to describe liberals trying to make lynching a federal crime."

"We have enough laws on the books. The states can handle themselves."

"No doubt the black citizens of Mississippi are applauding your high-minded position."

"I'm not totally in favor of extralegal executions, but there were only seven lynchings in the entire nation last year, which suggests the evil is being dealt with on a local level."

"Only seven? Then that should satisfy those poor, dead souls—and their grieving families."

"I'm beginning to think you may be a bleeding-heart liberal yourself, Mr. Tokoloshe."

"Which by default must make me an admirer of Franklin and Eleanor."

"Ah yes, Old Moosejaw and La Boca Grande. When Giuseppe Zangara attempted to murder Roosevelt in Miami five years ago, but shot the mayor of Chicago by mistake, clearly he assassinated the wrong man."

"Just why are you here tonight, Pegler? Café Society doesn't seem to be your kind of place. In fact, nothing in the Village does."

"I'm attempting to know the reds better so I can characterize them more accurately in my column. My five-million readers crave to be informed."

"And who's your little pal in the big suit?"

"Meet Herr Dedrick Leitner, originally from Germany, who is about to acquire his citizenship papers, and who wants to more suitably understand America's odd cultural tastes."

Leitner half rose, snapping his heels.

I said, "Then I'm sure Herr Leitner must be amused by the clever Hitler simulacrum suspended from the ceiling."

Leitner, in a noticeable German accent, said, "Even I appreciate a little Jewish humor from time to time."

I said, "Yeah, betcha old Adolph himself laughs at a good dirty joke—when he's out on the town with Göring, Goebbels, and the boys."

"Some may disparage Mr. Hitler, Mr. Tokoloshe," Pegler said, "but the Fuehrer is the only man alive who can save the world from Bolshevism, and, of course, he's getting the Jewish problem under control."

"What Jewish problem?"

"Even you aren't so naïve as to claim you don't know."

"No, Pegler, I don't know, not being Jewish or anything

else. I guess I'll just have to read your column to find out—assuming I find it sufficiently sanitary to handle the newsprint on which it's printed. *Auf Wiedersehen*."

I was in a near fury as Diana and I emerged from the smoky warren into the crisp, Manhattan night. She clutched my arm.

"Easy, Tokee, darling, catch your breath. You did superbly. Never blew your wig once."

"I did blow it. It just didn't tilt."

As we hunted for an uptown cab, she said, "Let me tell you something strange. I've seen that German man, Mr. Leitner, before. At the shop my seamstress operates on East Eighty-Second in Yorkville. Her name is Frieda Waxweiler, and she's sewing some of my own designs for me."

"Obviously, given her last name, she's German."

"Although she was born in The Bronx."

"Yorkville *is* the city's major German enclave."

"Not to ignore all the Hungarians, Czechoslovaks, and Poles who also live there."

"So you believe there's a peculiar connection between Waxweiler and Leitner?"

"Frieda only sews women's apparel, Tokee, and I've never seen a man in her shop—except him. There's something else that's odd. Every time I go in, I see lots of mail and packages from all over the globe. I can't help but notice that the mail comes from faraway places like Argentina, Uruguay, France, Holland, Spain. Frieda's a simple seamstress, a lovely older woman. Who would she know in all those countries?"

"Far-flung relatives maybe?"

"I'm often there when the postman delivers her mail, but I never see her give him anything to go out. Don't you find it odd?"

"You believe all this mail she gets has something to do with Leitner?"

"I think we ought to check it out. Especially in light of what's happening in the world."

Nineteen-thirty-eight was a bummer, shaping up abominably for global humanity. The Vatican formally recognized Franco's Fascists; Canton was overrun by Jap warlords; on so-called Kristallnacht Nazi scum burned and looted Jewish businesses and synagogues; the Wehrmacht marched into the Sudetenland. And while all that lunacy was going on, hapless Neville Chamberlain declared peace for our time after licking Hitler's ass.

A Checker stopped for us just as Orson Welles emerged from Café Society.

"Tokol, Diana," he called. "I'm headed uptown. May I share your cab?"

Slender and boyish, with a basso voice and just twenty-four, Orson had the whole city talking. He'd roared into New York to do Shakespeare, launched his own Mercury Theater company, and now was realizing serious stuff on the radio for Columbia, not to mention being the voice of Lamont Cranston on Mutual's "The Shadow."

Who knows what evil lurks in the hearts of man?

Welles sometimes went around town in a black hat, cape, and mask.

"You're a busy guy, Orson," I said as we settled into the cab.

"I'm talking to RKO about directing a movie. If it pans out I'll be in Hollywood next year. I know a lot of major-domos in the movie biz who think I'm not up to it, but I intend to prove them wrong."

"What's the movie about?"

"Something regarding a Machiavellian-like newspaper publisher, but I haven't decided yet. However, whatever it is will be magnificent."

"Spoken like a man of confidence," Diana said.

"My dear, nobody who takes on anything big and tough can afford to be modest."

He turned to the driver, saying, "Drop me off at the St. Regis Hotel on East Fifty-Fifth."

I said, "Say, don't you and your wife live on West Fifty-Seventh?"

Orson looked a little sheepish. "I, um, am going to see a friend before I return home." He paused. "Don't look at me like that, you two. If there hadn't been women we men would still be squatting in caves eating raw meat. We made civilization to impress our girlfriends."

As he exited the cab at the hotel, he said, "Why don't you both visit my Columbia studio on Madison Avenue on Halloween? I'm cooking up something special for 'The Mercury Theater on the Air,' sort of a radio prank."

"You won't tell us what it is?" Diana said.

"And spoil the surprise?"

The next morning at Diana's penthouse, we again pondered the oddity of the middle-aged seamstress in Yorkville and the German schlemiel in the big suit. It was small bore—based on the global turbulence of our decade, yet Diana and I enjoyed intrigue even if we had to invent our own.

She showed me the patterns she'd made for her new dress design, which Mrs. Waxweiler, a more than able seamstress, was working on.

"It'll be beautiful, Tokee, darling. My dress is designed to stretch sensually over the contours of the body, a silk crepe-de-chine draping across the grain at a forty-five degree angle with a minimal amount of darting."

"Hey, dollface, I have no idea what you're talking about, but on you it'll be a lollapalooza."

"I'm leaving now for another fitting, so when I get to Mrs. Waxweiler's I'll snoop around. If anything comes up I'll call your office from the payphone on Third Avenue under the Elevated around the corner from her shop."

It didn't take long. The phone rang the moment I walked into to my Chrysler Building suite.

"Grab a cab and get here quick, Tokee," Diana said. "Mr. Leitner is inside the shop."

While heading uptown to Yorkville, it entered my mind that perhaps there was no hanky panky, that Leitner and Waxweiler were just having a Teutonic-style, midlife fling. Maybe it was a bunch of hoo-ha on our part.

After I met up with Diana, we lurked in a doorway across from Waxweiler's.

"Tokee, I had almost finished my fitting when Mr. Leitner came in. He and Mrs. Waxweiler merely nodded to each other, and he just kind of hung around, obviously waiting for me to leave. As usual, I saw a lot of mail with foreign postmarks. When I went back into the dressing room to change, I peeked through the curtain and saw him gather up all the mail and put it into a valise. I phoned you as soon as I left the shop. He's been in there so long, I wonder what they're doing."

"Probably the dipsy doodle in the dressing room. Hold on, he's leaving—carrying the valise."

"Follow him, Tokee. Let's get to the bottom of this. I'll meet you back at the apartment."

Leitner turned the corner, and two-blocks north mounted the stairs of the IRT's 84th Street El. Perhaps overconfident, he seemed unaware he was being tailed.

After a five-car, south-bound, South Ferry local screeched into the station, he entered the second coach, while I got into the third. Riding between cars, I watched him through the end door. The noise was deafening, not only the squeal of wheel against rail, but the rattle and knock of the wooden cars.

As we lurched south, on either side of the track I saw into the open windows of the tenements, some so close I could almost grab the laundry flapping from the clotheslines. From some of those windows eyes glared back at me, and I felt as though I were an intruder, ogling private intimacies I had no right to observe. Tenement living was more of a blight than a blessing, despite the pathos of geraniums flowering on the windowsills.

Leitner got off the train at 53rd, and I followed as he left the El and walked west to 12th Avenue where he ducked into the aptly-named Hell's Kitchen Diner directly across from Pier 90—where the German cruise ship *Europa* was berthed.

Through the front window, I saw Leitner sitting in a booth across from a man dressed in a white, nautical uniform. I couldn't hear their conversation, but soon the ship's crewman, carrying the valise, left and walked across the street to the pier.

I decided to stick with Leitner, who headed to 42nd just west of Times Square and the Dixie, a middling hotel that shared space with the Central Union Bus terminal. The buses entered the basement via a ramp and onto a revolving platform so they could be turned. Inside the seven-hundred room hotel, I lost him. I didn't know if Leitner took a bus out of town or an elevator to a room. The desk clerk confirmed Leitner was a guest, registered in room nineteen-nineteen, a number I consigned to memory.

Back at Diana's, we compared notes.

"Tokee, I learned that Mrs. Waxweiler's late husband was

born in Dusseldorf, was a private in the German Army in the Great War, and that the two met in New York when he was sent here by his employer, a German electronics firm. I didn't ask about the foreign mail addressed to her. It might make her suspicious."

"And rightly so because Leitner gave all that mail to a crewmember of the *Europa*, which makes weekly crossings to Hamburg. Also, Leitner's shelling out two-and-a-half bucks a night for a room with private bath and radio at the Dixie Hotel.

"And all this tells us… what?"

"That Mrs. Waxweiler's shop is a mail-drop for Nazi spies."

"Although we're not at war with Germany."

"The Nazis are getting a head start."

"Okay, Tokee, what are we going to do about it?"

"I know an agent in the FBI's New York field office, Mike Litvak. He's not too bright, but he was born in Belarus, so he not only speaks Belarusian but German. Worked on the Lindbergh baby kidnapping and got an arm wound during that gangland massacre at Union Station in Kansas City. He's a high-profile agent. I'll run what we have past him."

Just that morning I read in the *Herald Tribune* that my old pal Clarence Darrow had died in Chicago, and wired my condolences to his widow Ruby. I hadn't seen him since I bailed him out of an extortion con in Illinois coal country. Darrow once spoke to the Associated Motion Picture Advertisers at a luncheon, coincidentally at the Dixie Hotel. The Hollywood studios had been coerced into adopting a ludicrous self-censorship code, which, among other things, prohibited excessive kissing and ridicule of the clergy, although not necessarily in that order. They even made Betty Boop change her short skirts. Darrow hated censorship in *any* form, as he made clear in his speech.

Shouting came easily to Mike Litvak, who wanted to become more famous in FBI annals than Melvin Purvis, the agent who shot Dillinger. Mike and I had something in common. We both despised J. Edgar Hoover.

"Damn it, Tokol," he roared when I met him at the agency's downtown field office. "You might have blown our whole operation—if we actually had one."

"You know about Leitner and Waxweiler?"

"Waxweiler, no. But I've had Leitner in my sights. His name came up when an MI6 operative in Bremen uncovered some compromising papers involving the Gestapo. Problem is, there's nothing we can pin on him."

"I met Leitner the other night at Café Society, Mike. He gives every impression of being an idiot. And if he's a spy he's a klutz."

"I suspect it was Leitner who phoned the Manhattan Passport Office alleging to be a Mr. Jones, assistant to Secretary of State Cordell Hull. The caller demanded that fifty blank passports be hand-delivered to him at a room at the Dixie Hotel. Spies can do a lot with a blank passport.

"Naturally, the passport clerk was suspicious, checked with Hull's office, found there was no such assistant, and called the NYPD. When the cops went to the room of this so-called Jones—surprise!—it was empty."

"An obvious and stupid con, Mike."

"I think it was a test run for a bigger and better scam at the same hotel. This time, someone claiming to be a Colonel Smith, aide de camp to the Third Army Corps's commanding general, phoned Fort Totten in Willets Point and spoke to one of the staff, Lieutenant Walters.

"This Smith, no doubt Leitner, ordered Walters to bring

classified papers about American coastal defenses to an emergency military meeting at, yes, the Dixie, room fourteen-twelve. Walters was instructed to tell no one. Since caller had a foreign accent, the lieutenant, being skeptical, phoned us."

"You guys will be there when Walters and this so-called Smith meet, right?"

"Wrong. Hoover's put the kibosh on it. Claims there are too many jurisdictional issues. War Department, Army, NYPD, State Department. He's keeping the FBI out of it. And me in particular."

"So Leitner, an obvious Nazi spy practically begging to be arrested, will be sitting in a room at the Dixie waiting for classified info to be dumped on his lap. And you bums won't be there to bust the bastard?"

"That's about the size of it."

"Such a crock. Mike, *I'll* go as Lieutenant Walters."

"You?"

"Why not? If the FBI's not interested in capturing a Nazi spy I am."

"But you said Leitner knows you."

"We only met once. I'll wear a disguise."

"Then what?"

"I'll take care of Leitner in my own way."

"Tokol, you know the FBI can't back you up. I gotta lay low on this. Hoover's been riding my ass, claims I'm getting more publicity than he is. Listen, I'll try to be there, unofficially, but if anything goes wrong you're on your own."

"I've got Diana. She's a match for any Nazi. Mike, make me photostats of some nautical charts, the kind publicly available from any marine shop. I need to take something that looks halfway legit."

We shook on it.

For years, I had been playing the alhaita, an African double-reed wind instrument I took up under the tutelage of Nigerian prince Gabriel Momodu, who became a chum during my diamond-dealing days. The oboe-like alhaita was a bitch to master, but by Western standards my playing was… Well, even it if was lousy who in the States would know?

New York needed me and my alhaita. The city hadn't been the same since LaGuardia banned the hurdy-gurdy men. Why? The half-Italian mayor was embarrassed by organ grinders from Naples dispatching monkeys with funny hats and tin cups to beg for coins.

My confrontation with Leitner at the Dixie wasn't until the next afternoon, so in formal dress I packed my alhaita and went to Carnegie Hall where Benny Goodman and his band were setting up for a major jazz concert. I met Benny through Diana when she worked with NBC's "Let's Dance" and Benny was making his mark as The King of Swing. Benny was one smart cookie, so no wonder his show was sponsored by the National Biscuit Company.

Dressed in white tie and tails, Benny said, "Hey, Tokol, I see you brought your alhaita. You going to sit in with us tonight?"

"That's the idea, if you'll have me."

"I'll seat you in the wind section with Ziggy Elman, Harry James, Art Rollin, Babe Russin, and Hymie Schertzer."

"You're aces with me, pal."

"I guess you know our repertoire."

"By heart."

"I've been trying to get some of the band to learn the alhaita, but it's too hard for them. What's the secret?"

"Simple. Superior lung capacity, breathing from the diaphragm, and spine stabilization. Squats and weightlifting help too."

"Hmmm, let me write that down."

"Say, Benny, isn't Carnegie Hall an unusual venue for you?"

"Yeah, there are lots of highbrows who don't cotton to swing, so I'm a little nervous."

"But you always look so relaxed up on stage."

"Relaxed, my elbow. It's practice. Isn't that how you get to Carnegie Hall?"

Benny had nothing to worry about. Every seat was sold out—even though the best ones were priced at a near prohibitive two bucks seventy-five. The place rocked with wild applause and dancing in the aisles, especially during my alhaita solo on "Sing, Sing, Sing" backed by Gene Krupa on the tubs.

Although exhilarated by the music, I slept poorly that night, tossing and turning. It had been four years since we put The Man With Two Faces into the ground, but rarely was there a night that Janus hadn't returned to haunt me in my dreams. Some of those hallucinogenic visions were so vivid that his murderous anger and rage felt almost tactile, and yet his visitations would not cease until I cried out in my sleep. Diana would hold me saying, "Tokee, it's all right. Janus is gone now."

Although exhausted after the Goodman concert, and my lack of sleep, I was as prepared as I could be for my confrontation with Dedrick Leitner in room fourteen-twelve of the Dixie Hotel.

As Lieutenant Walters, I was smartly dressed in breeches, boots, military tunic emblazoned with medals, and a riding crop under my arm. With a thin mustache under my nose and peaked visor hat on my head, it was unlikely the Kraut would recognize me.

Okay, I might have slightly overdone it with the riding crop.

Although he had claimed in his phony call that he was the commanding general's top aide, Leitner wasn't in uniform himself, which was no surprise. The little shit wore the same over-sized suit he had on that night at Café Society. Like a good officer I saluted anyway.

"Did you bring the papers, Lieutenant Walters?"

"Indeed, Colonel Smith, just as you asked. They're top secret, sir. Should they fall into the wrong hands..."

"That will be all, Lieutenant," he said taking from my hand the envelope with the nautical charts.

"Sir, I thought this was an emergency staff meeting, but I see no one else here."

Holding the papers in one hand, with the other he pulled a Luger from his coat.

"Raise your hands, *schweinhund*."

"I'm beginning to think I've been misled, Colonel."

"Colonel, *mein arsch*. You Americans are not only decadent with your jazz, your comic strips, your radio quiz shows, and your silly Hollywood movies, but you are all *dummkopfs*, as we say in Dortmund. Now march to the toilet."

"But I don't have to go."

"Better I shoot you dead in the tub rather than to make more work for the maid. I like to be tidy. It is a family trait."

"Why are you going to shoot me?"

"To leave no witnesses to our little transaction."

With the Luger he motioned toward the bathroom door. Naturally, I obeyed. Who'd want to mess up the floor of the Dixie Hotel with a little blood?

Inside the claustrophobic bathroom, he ordered me to

climb into the tub.

"May I wash my hands first?"

"Why?"

"It's part of my religion. We always clean ourselves properly before saying our prayers."

"Then do it, but quick. *Schnell*!"

I ran the water in the sink. It came out slow and rusty. Dribble, dribble, dribble. As the water sluggishly filled the sink, Leitner grew impatient.

"Enough," he said finally. "I am not waiting. Open your mouth."

"Huh?"

"You heard me."

I did as ordered. He placed the gun barrel in my mouth, not deep, but far enough for me to know that a bullet was about to enter my brain through my palate.

But one thing the moron forgot. The riding crop under my arm. To use it I had to get close to him, and the tiny bathroom was ideal.

In the blink of an eye, as we stood next to the trickling faucet, I jerked my head away from the gun while pivoting the crop, bringing it up hard on Leitner's gun hand. The Luger went off, just past my ear, but the bullet thudded harmlessly into the ceiling.

Damn, that shot was loud. My ear was ringing.

Leitner was no more accomplished as an assassin than he was as a spy.

I continued to make decent use of the riding crop, giving the bastard more than a few good whacks as I wrestled the gun away. As he cowered into a pathetic Germanic ball on the floor, I was tempted finish him off with his own Luger. But I figured Litvak might want to ask a few questions of an actual, breathing Nazi spy.

Mike and Diana burst into the room.

Diana said, "We heard the shot, Tokee. Are you all right?"

"It was a piece of strudel."

I shut off the faucet, and we dragged Leitner out of the jon, plopping him into a chair. I peeled the mustache from my upper lip.

He said, "You, you… I know you. From that degenerate place of jazz, all those black and white people mingling together. And so many Hebrews."

"You'll have to tell your boyfriend Pegler how we met up again. It might even make his column. Especially the part about my lifting your Luger."

"Execute me. I am prepared."

Litvak moved in and identified himself.

"Call me Agent Mike, Herr Leitner. No one's going to execute you. I'd just like to ask you a few simple questions, if you don't mind. I hope you can spare the time."

"Well…"

"*Ich spreche Deutsch.*"

"*Ja?*"

"*Wie geht es deine Mutter?*" Mike said, asking about Leitner's mother.

"*Sie ist eine Hündin,*" Leitner replied, characterizing his mom as a bitch.

"Sorry to hear that. Say, do you need anything, Mr. Leitner? Tokol, how about getting him a glass of water? No, I've a better idea. Something from the bar downstairs. What would you like, Mr. Leitner? Anything at all. It's on the FBI."

"Perhaps a glass of schnapps?"

"Done. Tokol, Diana, will you do Mr. Leitner the honors?"

Diana went to get the schnapps, while Mike, in true ass-kissing form, cozied up to Leitner.

"That was such a clever stunt you pulled, Mr. Leitner. Or may I call you Dedrick?"

"Not too clever, it seems. You caught me."

"Oh, we just got lucky. It takes a man of rare intelligence such as yourself to conceive of something like this—as well as daring."

"Really?"

"It's not easy being a spy. I know from personal experience."

"Yes, very difficult. Especially when you are not appreciated in Berlin."

"I truly understand, Dedrick. It's the bureaucracy, right?"

"I am scorned and paid poorly by the Abwehr, our intelligence division. The chief, Wilhelm Canaris, treats me like *schmutz*."

"It happens here too. We have a man like that named Hoover. I bet all the other spies you work with here in the States feel the same way you do."

"*Nein*, they are too stupid. All they know is obedience. They never take the initiative. It was I who thought about luring your lieutenant to the hotel with those classified papers."

"And you might have succeeded. You were so close. But it wasn't your fault. Circumstances, that's all. Could have happened to anyone."

"I feel like a mere delivery boy. Every week it falls on me to lug a load of mail to the *Europa*. I am not a mailman. I am educated as a metallurgist. Also, I have to keep buying valises."

"It's demeaning, Dedrick. I know how you feel. Say, who at the *Europa* takes the mail off your hands?"

"A purser, Josef Jaeger, is our courier. He personally delivers it to the Abwehr in Germany."

"And this mail comes from…"

"Our agents around the world. Vital intelligence information."

"So instead of mailing it directly to Berlin, where it might be intercepted en route, your agents send it to Mrs. Frieda Waxweiler."

"She is a nice, lovely seamstress. Who would ever suspect her? Or open her mail?"

"And you collect the mail regularly from her shop."

"Yes, but I am also, as you say in America, fucking her."

"Dedrick, I'm sure there's no Nazi spy in the States as dedicated to his craft as you. How many are there, by the way?"

"Twenty. Many of them here in New York."

"Do they all report to you?"

He laughed. "*Nein*, I am not important enough."

"Don't depreciate yourself, Dedrick. I'm sure you're much more essential than you think. Just who is it they report to?"

"Dr. Ignatz Griebl."

"And he is…?"

"An obstetrician. His office is on East Eighty-Sixth."

"You've certainly been helpful, Dedrick."

"I do not like the thought of being tortured, Agent Mike."

"Torture never crossed my mind. Ah, Diana's back with your schnapps. Drink up, my *freund*. I speak for J. Edgar Hoover when I say America is grateful to you."

"You will not shoot me?"

"Gracious me, perish the thought."

"Or put me in prison?"

"That's not entirely in my hands, Dedrick, but I assure you you'll receive the utmost consideration. Besides, our federal prisons are like country clubs. Golf, tennis, exquisite cuisine, fine wines, maid service. But I'm sure it'll never come to that. By the way, would you happen to have the names of all the German agents who report to Dr. Griebl?"

"*Jawohl.* I can give you their addresses too. And their places of work. Aircraft companies, shipyards, electronic facilities, tool plants."

"Say, I'd love to invite you as the FBI's guest to Lüchow's on East Fourteenth Street. I hear its German food is finer than any in Yorkville, that the wiener schnitzel is divine, and the pumpernickel is superior to Stuttgart's. We can continue our chat there. We have so much more to talk about."

"You are most generous, Agent Mike. Uh, if you don't mind, may I please have my Luger back? It belonged to my mother who fired it only on Sundays."

"Now, Dedrick, that might not be such a good idea. Tell you what. I'll personally hold on to your Luger and return it to you when the time is right. I hope you understand."

Leaving Leitner to finish his schnapps, guarded by Diana armed with her blowgun, Litvak and I conferred in the hall just outside the door.

"Mike, I almost had a fit, you were so damned obsequious to that Nazi shit."

"Paid off, didn't it? He's singing like a canary."

"He was gonna kill me, and he wants his pistol back?"

"In his dreams."

"Mike, you've practically got the entire Nazi spy network in America laid out for you. Hoover's gotta climb on board now."

"Maybe—after I take down this Griebl guy. But Hoover an obstinate prick. Plus I need to interest George Medalie. He's the U.S. Attorney for the Southern District."

"Is Leitner's word enough to prosecute Griebl and the rest

after you nab them?"

"We'll have to give them polygraphs."

"They say lie detectors aren't reliable."

"Madmen, imbeciles, and women in heat can beat 'em, but they're good enough for an espionage indictment under Section Thirty-two of Title Fifty of the U.S. Code. You know what I'm going to do, Tokol? Tip Walter Winchell about the spy probe and plant scuttlebutt in the *New York Post*. I know a guy there. A little press will put the heat on Hoover and his yes men."

"Not a good idea, Mike. Maybe you ought to keep it hush-hush until it's a sure thing."

"If I wait, the investigation might be taken out of my hands and given to someone who'll blow it. There's no sense of emergency at the bureau. After all, being a Nazi or a commie is no more of a crime than being a Republican."

"Maybe even less."

"Okay, Tokol, let's collect our pile of Germanic crap and head to Lüchow's for a Teutonic high time. On Hoover."

Diana and I begged off. We'd done our duty. Besides, Orson Welles's "Mercury Theater On the Air" was being broadcast live that night, and we'd promised to be there.

The show, lacking a sponsor, was up against serious competition from NBC's Edgar Bergen and Charlie McCarthy under the aegis of Chase & Sanborn. Orson broadcast from the nondescript Columbia studios at 485 Madison Avenue, where we were ushered into Studio One. The show had no studio audience, but Welles seated us in folding chairs in the corner.

"I want you two to actually have a part on the show," he told us.

Diana asked Orson for a copy of the script. She was, after

all, the doyen of the networks' most lucrative soap operas.

"You don't need a script, my dear. On my cue I want you both to scream off mike at the tops of your lungs—just as if you were being roasted alive by aliens from outer space."

The tension was palpable as the studio orchestra directed by Bernard Herrmann took its place, the actors and technicians darting about rattling their scripts, the sound effects guys, one of whom was an old friend of Diana's named Larry, testing their acoustical marvels. Then all went silent as the on-air light flashed and announcer Dan Seymour intoned, "The Columbia Broadcasting System and its affiliated stations present Orson Welles and the Mercury Theater On the Air in *The War of the Worlds* by H.G. Wells."

While melodramatic, the script was relatively arresting, particularly when the Martian invasion of New Jersey was described by actors portraying reporters being incinerated while voicing live remotes. Orson played three roles: host, narrator, and a professor named Pierson. I was superb shrieking in my radio debut, although it left my voice hoarse. Diana was a pro at screaming as she tended to be noisy while enjoying sex. An hour after it began, Orson concluded the show by announcing that the performance had no further significance, and was merely his way of dressing up in a sheet and jumping out of a bush and going boo.

Suddenly, just as the on-air light flicked off, the studio door burst open and in rushed a bevy of uniformed cops, herding the performers, including Diana and me, against a wall, and gathering up all the scripts from the floor.

A police lieutenant told Welles, "You're being held for investigation, sir. Have you any idea the panic you caused? The thousands of deaths and suicides, that deadly stampede in a Jersey fraternal hall, the fatal traffic crashes? You have a lot to answer for."

Orson, a wide-eyed innocent, said, "Me?"

Eventually we were released, and Diana and I, in the company of Orson's sound effects guy, Larry, left the building by a back exit to escape the horde of reporters in front.

Outside, however, there was no panic in the air, and Madison Avenue was its usual midnight self. Save for the Times Square theater district, Manhattan was often eerie at night. Neighborhoods teeming with people during the day would turn empty and silent, the denizens either ensconced in their protective warrens or spirited away by Martians.

Larry, Diana, and I got back to her penthouse wondering what all the fuss had been about. As the three of us dove into Diana's huge circular bed, she said, "Larry, let's hear some of those wonderful animal noises you make on the air.

Larry accommodated us with a roar, then a growl, snort, squeal, bark, caw, concluding with a bellow, and, after the three of were sweaty and done, a gentle purr.

It turned out there were no deaths or suicides. Nevertheless, Orson was publicly contrite. But when asked if he should have toned the violence in the show, he said, "No, you don't play murder in soft words."

The following week, Walter Winchell went on the air with a scoop:

Good evening, Mr. and Mrs. America and all the ships at sea. Let's go to press. Flash! This reporter has learned exclusively that a federal grand jury is about to investigate a major Nazi spy ring. As many as twenty Nazi agents in New York, Boston, Buffalo, and Philadelphia are under surveillance, including a Dr. Ignatz Griebl of Yorkville. So far, one spy is in custody as a cooperating witness.

A similar story appeared in the *New York Post*.

Agent Mike's handiwork.

A few days later I met Litvak at the bar at Jack and Charlie's, the former speakeasy at 21 W. 52nd. Mike was sleep-
needy and depressed.

"I'm not drinking," he said, "so I'll just have a Manhattan,
no ice, and lose the cherry."

"What's wrong, Mike?"

"Hoover fired my ass."

"What the hell? You were on to something big."

"Thanks to you and Diana. I almost caught Griebl, but
just as we were about to close in he split the country on the
Europa. All the other spies escaped too. As for Leitner, we
have no one for him to testify against, and since we offered
him immunity he's scot-free."

"How did all this happen?"

"Those leaks I gave to Winchell and the *Post* tipped off
the bad guys, and they fled before I could nab them."

"Not the smartest thing to do. I tried to—"

"Yeah, yeah. I shoulda listened. So Hoover canned me
for violating the G-man's oath: no agent may disclose service
information."

"Pretty obvious you were the leaker."

"I thought I had the right to use any dope I got from my
own investigations personally."

"Hoover disagreed."

"He showed me the contract I signed."

"And Mrs. Waxweiler?"

"She was just a dupe, in love with the Nazi who was
schtupping her."

"Look at it like this, Mike. The Nazis will be around for
a while. There'll be plenty more spies to bust in the future."

"Without me. My brother-in-law got me a job in security

at Wanamaker's Department Store in Philly. Now I'll be investigating shoplifters."

Flash! This reporter has learned that the captain of the German cruise ship Europa *has been taken into custody as a material witness and is being held on twenty-five-hundred dollars bail. Captain Franz Boehnke is suspected of allowing Nazi couriers to use the* Europa *to relay espionage information to the Abwehr in Berlin. Meanwhile, the German-American Bund continues its Nazi propaganda crusade unchecked here in the Land of the Free.*

Flash! Your reporter has learned exclusively that something's not kosher at the World's Fair in Flushing Meadow, and it involves a threat to destroy one of the international pavilions. By whom and how cannot be revealed at this time, but I can say that my heroic Certain Acquaintance is on the case—even at the risk to his own personal safety.

…For Jergens Lotion, this is Walter Winchell wishing you lotions of love.

six

World's Fair 1939

It was the year I became a storm trooper for the German American Bund.

The waters of the Lagoon of Nations glowed yellow as a modest preamble before erupting into polychromatic geysers from a thousand nozzles. Streaks of fire from four-hundred gas jets were preceded by billows of multicolored mist. Three-hundred-fifty firework launchers thunderously ignited the sky in a nightly pyrotechnic display over the World's Fair.

As millions of visitors flocked to Flushing Meadows, Queens, a National Jewish Council delegation led by Isadore Greenbaum called on Tokoloshe and Son Cleansing Services in the Chrysler Building, begging me to bring down Bund Fuehrer Fritz Kuhn. The war to succeed the War to End All Wars had begun in Europe, even as FDR dismissed spurious rumors about returning American boys to European fields.

"Mr. Tokoloshe," Greenbaum said, "the plight of European Jews has become intolerable. Our own government turned from our shores the *St. Louis*, an outcast ship carrying more than nine-hundred Jewish refugees, forcing them back to Europe to face an uncertain fate."

"A disgrace and a humanitarian tragedy, but why come to me?"

"We know you were involved in exposing that Nazi spy ring last year."

"Nonsense, Mr. Greenbaum, and if you think I had anything to do with it we might as well be playing tiddlywinks with manhole covers."

"We have our sources."

"A source named Winchell, perchance? Man never could keep his crevice closed. But I don't know how I can be of help to you."

"The German American Bund is an arm of the Nazi Party. Join it. See if you can destroy it from inside and wreck Kuhn."

"Oh sure. That'll be a snap. I'll hop on it right away."

"You're being facetious, Mr. Tokoloshe."

"Of course I am, yet... Y'know, the idea kind of intrigues me."

I tended to make snap decisions. Particularly if the principle seemed appropriate. And this seemed to be the right proposition at the right time. Diana would approve. Or not.

"Okay, Mr. Greenbaum, I'll do it. I enjoy a challenge."

So much so, I waived my usual fee.

After flirting with careers as a tightrope walker, brain surgeon, ukulele professional, Tower of London Beefeater, and horse chiropractor I had found my calling.

I phonied-up my credentials and joined the Bund, managing to ingratiate myself with Heinz Hinrichs, head of Bund security. To the Bund I was one Rolfe Schenk of Milwaukee, certified anti-Semite, ardent admirer of Adolph Hitler, and willing to do heavy lifting—even if it meant cracking non-Aryan skulls. The Germans welcomed me as a probationary storm trooper, and quickly I found that Hinrichs was my key to Fritz Kuhn.

I disguised myself, of course, using a little toothbrush mustache under my nose, my hair combed unflatteringly in a demonic way.

Hinrichs said, "My God, Rolfe, you look just like—"

"I know. Charlie Chaplin."

Diana played along as my kissing cousin Elke Bachmeier. We went to Bund dances at the Lorelei dance hall, picnics at Camp Nortland on winsome Lake Iliff in New Jersey, and Hudson River outings to West Point.

As a casual drinking *freund* of Hinrichs I used every opportunity to get him plastered on schnapps, beer, and ale at Alfons Rambacher's Bierstube on East 86th in Yorkville.

Hinrichs said, "Rolfe, having Lindy at the rally would be a hell of a coup. He is a champion for both Germans and Americans, and his views count."

Gossip was rife that Charles A. Lindbergh would pay a surprise visit to the upcoming German American Bund rally at Madison Square Garden, which would lend a certain cachet to the event. However, once called the Lone Eagle for his intrepid aeronautics, he was now dismissed as the Lone Ostrich by Water Winchell.

"Heinz, Lindbergh's a Swede. He can't be a member of the Bund unless he's a true German American. Like us."

"Then we will make him an honorary member. Lindy has visited Germany, understands the Nazi military is invincible, was awarded the Service Cross of the German Eagle, and he believes that if the Jews have their way they will lead America into war. A few Yids are all right, but too many create chaos, and we are getting too many."

"You said it, Heinz. Praise the Lord our Fuehrer is doing something about it."

"I will drink to that. *Zum wohl.*"

While Hinrichs was an enthusiast of all things Nazi, he was no fan of Kuhn. As we funneled the booze down our throats, his lips loosened.

"I have tried to work with Fritz, but he is a *stechen*, as we say in Stuttgart."

"Yeah, I've met a lot of pricks myself."

"*Gut*, Rolfe, you know our language good."

"I was bred in Milwaukee—and I did spend a little time in Hamburg. Wo *ist die toilette?*"

"The important thing is I do not think Kuhn is—how you say it?—on the up and up."

"In what way, Heinz?"

"Because… Uh, I had better clam up about that. Say, it is getting late. Let us order a schooner to go with our schnapps."

Pretty soon we were singing "The Horst Wessel Song," and the entire schnockered crowd at Rambacher's Bierstube joined in.

The cacophony accosted the very sidewalks of Sauerkraut Boulevard, heart of America's Deutschland, where the tenements were lined with Teutonic bustle and *musik*: Café Geiger, Maxi's Bauhaus, Martin's Rathskeller, Mueller's Pork Store, Bavarian Inn, the Heidelberg, Kleine Konditorei, Café Wienecke, Platzl Café, Wankel's Hardware.

The marzipan at Elk Candy was delicious.

As for Kuhn, a naturalized American citizen and former chemical engineer, I was worming my way closer, thanks to my palsy-walsy relationship with Heinz, who made the introductions at Bund headquarters in Room 5, 178 E. 85th Street, where they published their newspaper, the eight-page *Free American*.

Kuhn, stocky and pasty-faced with a noticeable accent, peered into me through his wire-rimmed glasses.

"Heinz tells me you have a background in security, Herr Schenk."

"Call me Rolfe, sir. I was once a doorman at T.A. Chap-

man's Department Store on Wisconsin Avenue in Milwaukee."

"Why did you join our Bund?"

"I desire the unification of all those of German descent,
regardless of the sovereignty in which they are domiciled. The
Bund alone recognizes the aspirations of our racial comrades
to remove the barriers in our path. The *weltanschauung* of the
Third Reich, with its lofty ideals, forms a trenchant contrast to
the liberalistic capitalistic philosophy under which we exist in
America."

"*Das ist gut.* I could not have said it better."

So true. Kuhn himself had mouthed those pompous words
in a speech published in his little Nazi propaganda sheet.

"You and I are of like mind," he said. "We cherish sympa-
thies for the greatness of the Reich, and we must stand like
men before Herr Hitler and thank him for saving our Deutschland from that bloody, Godless Asiatic monster called Jewish
Communism. There are thirty-million Germans living in the
United States, Rolfe, and they must assert the rights of their
blood by every and any means while preparing for the coming
struggle with Communism and Jews. *Sieg Heil!*"

"*Sieg Heil!*"

It took me zero seconds to detest Kuhn and everything he
stood for.

From the unguarded coat rack at Bund headquarters, I
swiped the name tag from inside his hat, pinning the label
on the twenty-five-cent rag doll I bought for a hundred bucks
from Mambo Miriam, the voodoo queen on Chartres Street
in New Orleans. Daily I'd stick an additional pin into the devil
doll, but so far I hadn't seen any changes in Kuhn's health.

I was beginning to think voodoo might be a fraud.

When the day came for the rally, tensions were rampant

inside and out of Madison Square Garden. Twenty-two-thousand Bundists and their abettors crammed the arena, while on the streets enclosing Eighth and Ninth avenues, one-hundred-thousand anti-Fascists were in a righteous fervor.

As one of the uniformed storm troopers in the hall, I was dressed for the part: brown shirt, armband with SS insignia, cuffless dark trousers, black overseas cap, Sam Brown belt, and brass knuckles in my pocket. Looked pretty good, actually—if you weren't bothered by the gladiatorial attire of despots.

Diana was a sucker for a man in uniform, and got wet and feverish whenever the United Parcel guy dropped off a package. One priceless night, while in the background Xavier Cugat's band played rumbas in a radio remote from the Waldorf Astoria, Diana insisted I wear my SS uniform in bed. However, she drew the line at my brass knuckles.

"Too lumpy," she complained. "Chuck 'em, Tokee."

A pity Diana, who enjoyed a good scrap, had to skip the rally. She was working at the RCA Pavilion at the World's Fair as NBC's Miss Television. While Diana was the progenitor of radio's most popular soap operas, slave-driving a covey of hack writers, she saw the limitless possibilities of launching her shows on the little home screen, whenever television became a practicality.

The assembly at the Garden was kicked off by a Nazi drum and bugle corps made up of darling eight and nine year olds garbed in white shirts, brown kerchiefs, dark blue shorts, Sam Brown belts, and Basque berets. The little girls wore the same except for skirts. Nazi babies were adorable. Unfortunately, they grew up. Like cats.

As Heinz Hinrichs and I guarded the stage, he lamented, "Seems like Lindbergh is a no-show, Rolfe."

"Doesn't appear to have hurt enthusiasm. Looks to me

like there's a German ass in every seat."

A gigantic full-body portrait of George Washington flanked by American flags dominated the stage, while from the mezzanine dangled a banner with the nifty slogan, STOP JEWISH DOMINATION OF CHRISTIAN AMERICANS. Why didn't I think of that?

Swastikas fluttered like buzzard's wings.

After "The Star-Spangled Banner," Fritz Kuhn mounted the stage to exuberant one-arm Nazi salutes, a standing ovation, and a drum corps's relentless thrum, thrum, thrum.

"You have all heard of me through the Jewish-controlled press as a creature with horns, cloven hoof, and a long tail. They will tell you I am putting on a hocus pocus, that what I say is propaganda from Herr Goebbels. As if no German-American is allowed to express an opinion that does not conform to the standardized order."

Kuhn went on to attack FDR as Frank D. Rosenfeld and condemn what he called the Jew Deal.

Suddenly, he was interrupted by a heretic who rushed the stage. It was an almost suicidal act, the podium surrounded by jackbooted Krauts. How a protestor could even infiltrate the hall was hard to fathom. As the interloper was savagely beaten and kicked, his trousers ripped off, I joined the melee hoping to minimize his injuries, and when I pulled him into the clear I saw that he was Isadore Greenbaum of the National Jewish Council.

Despite my disguise he recognized me through his blood and tears, but was quick-witted enough not to show it. Before Greenbaum could suffer even more grievous injuries, the cops moved in and dragged him in handcuffs to a paddy wagon.

Hinrichs said to me, "Guess we showed that kike, huh, Rolfe?"

"Yeah, poor bastard never stood a chance."

The speeches resumed, and the nonsense and invective were like crossed signals from an Atwater Kent.

Spiritual rebirth of the German people…renewing Germanism on a racial basis…homage to our leader, savior of the world against Bolshevism…great American liberation movement under the swastika…service of the blood is our iron law… undue influence of Jewish-inspired British imperialism…preservation of our Germandom in the USA…assert the rights of our blood by every and any means…

Not once did I hear a word about peace, love, hope, equality, charity, understanding. For those I'd need to turn to Father Coughlin.

I noticed the columnist Dorothy Thompson, wife of my novelist buddy Sinclair Lewis, being dragged from the press box by storm troopers. I learned later she was given the bum's rush because she'd burst into laughter, intending to show how loony it was to take Bundists seriously.

Outside the Garden, seventeen-hundred cops, many astride horses, kept apart Nazi-adherents and protestors, who included Jewish mobsters Meyer Lansky, Bugsy Siegel, and Mickey Cohen. Who knew Jewish racketeers had a good side? Despite the throng, there were only thirteen arrests and just eight injuries.

As for Isadore Greenbaum, once he was patched up he was sentenced to twenty-five dollars or ten days in the can for disorderly conduct. Anonymously, Tokoloshe and Son Cleansing Services paid his fine.

Hinrichs and I celebrated the Bund's tour de force at Schweinsteiger's Rathskeller with a passel of fellow stormers. Their coarse, guttural voices rankled like a squall of roosters and hens. If the Nazis needed a language, they'd never find one more glottal and ugly than German. As usual, the alcohol flowed, and predictably Heinz got drunker by the drop.

Taking him aside, I said, allowing my own words to slur in solidarity, "You were telling me about Kuhn not being on the up and up…"

"Yes, but I cannot say nothing about it, because I could get into much trouble."

"You're with friends now, Heinz."

"All I can say is Kuhn is stealing from the Bund, like it is his private pirate chest. But there is something even bigger about to blow, although I cannot say nothing about that either."

"C'mon, Heinz, you know me. I ain't gonna blab."

"I am not telling, except to say it is going happen late on Tuesday at one of the international pavilions at the World's Fair."

"Which one?"

"My mouth is shut. But when it occurs it will be pip-pip and cheerio, old chap."

That's all I got out of Hinrichs before he passed out.

Whichever pavilion it was, it wouldn't be Germany's. There wasn't one. Hitler was too busy getting his rocks off from his shooting match in Europe to invest in a fair, particularly after LaGuardia proposed a Hall of Horrors dedicated to the Nazis. This outraged the Heinies who called the mayor a dirty little Talmud Jew.

RCA's pavilion was shaped like a vacuum tube. It's where Diana worked the floor as Miss Television, greeting visitors and explaining the wonders of the unfolding television era. To enter the pavilion and its Radio Living Room of Tomorrow, visitors passed a television set, the TRK-12, housed in a unique transparent cabinet, which displayed all its electronic guts.

Most visitors, including myself, had never actually seen a television screen before—except in the pages of *Radio-Craft*, the magazine published by Hugo Gernsback, the one who coined the term "television." But Gernsback was dubbed Hugo the Rat by his writers, who complained bitterly about his low rates, if he paid them at all.

Diana was at her stylish best as she led the curious to a bank of closed-circuit receivers picking up live images of the waving crowds outside the hall. She passed out cards as souvenirs reading, I WAS TELEVISED, which to me sounded faintly carnal.

Dumont, Westinghouse, and GE offered competing television exhibits, but mighty RCA, the rajah of radio, was the champ at touting the tube. Alas, there was but one station, W2XBS—video 45.25 mHz, audio 49.75 mHz.

"Tokee, darling, I was wondering when you would get here," Diana said, leaving a lipstick smudge on my cheek.

I was sans my nose beard.

"Got something important to tell you, dollface. I think the Nazis are about to—"

"Now's not the time, darling. I'm not only terribly busy, but you *must* meet David. His limo's waiting to return to him the city, so his schedule is tight."

"Who's David?"

Diana waved to a distinguished, balding, rather heavyset man, who waved back. Taking me by the hand, she led me through the crowd to where he stood magisterially.

"David, I'd like you to meet my fiancé, Tokol Tokoloshe. Tokee, this is David Sarnoff."

For a moment I was speechless. I'd just been introduced to the man who bossed the world's most powerful network.

Recapturing my wits, I said, "Mr. Sarnoff, without you radio wouldn't be radio."

"Marconi had a little to do with it, Mr. Tokoloshe."

"Tokol, if you will. And now *television*?"

"Ten years ago, Vladimir Zworykin showed me a cathode ray picture tube he invented called the kinescope, so I put him in charge of RCA's television technology. He's why we're in this pavilion today."

"Skeptics are saying television's an expensive fad."

"They said the same about the talkies Tokol. It's a beginning. When Roosevelt opened the fair, his speech was carried live on television, a historic first."

"What were his Crossley ratings?"

Sarnoff laughed. "The president may not have had many viewers, and Albert Einstein's speech likewise, but it was a milestone. Bloomingdale's and Wanamaker's are already selling four models including a tabletop. W2XBS broadcasts only an hour a day—and sets cost... Well, I won't say."

"I will, sir. Six-hundred dollars. Who in America can afford that?"

"But I intend to bring prices down until there's a television in every home. People crave visual images."

"Mr. Sarnoff, if it's images, we've got lots of picture magazines: *Life, Look, Pic, Click, See*. What's wrong with them?"

"They don't move."

"And what about this war business in Europe?"

"If we do get into the conflict—and FDR assures us we won't—commercial television might be slightly delayed. But if war's declared, I intend to enlist in the Signal Corps as a brigadier general."

Sarnoff shook my hand.

"Take good care of Miss Television here, Tokol. You're a lucky man."

Sarnoff went on his way, while Diana cornered Vladimir Zworykin.

"Tokee, let me introduce you to my friend Vlad."

Zworykin and Diana showed me around the RCA Pavilion, which displayed Vlad's various experimental camera and picture tubes, a receiver that projected images onto a large screen, a useless gadget called a facsimile machine, and a collection of sleek cabinetry integrating electronic components into a room's décor.

Looking down on it all was a huge statue of Nipper, the terrier mutt on Victor phonographs listening to his master's voice.

Diana said, "Tokee, darling, when I'm finished here I'll meet you at Le Restaurant du Pavilion de France overlooking the Lagoon of Nations. The entire staff was brought from Paris on the *Normandie*. You'll adore their menu. Stuffed artichokes, lobster *américaine* with added cream, and cold capon in tarragon aspic. Or we could grab a hot dog and sit on a bench somewhere."

I wandered through the fair, all flowers and fountains and marchers and musicians, sprawling over a three-mile expanse. It would take days to see it all.

The decade had been one of unrelenting gloom, from the dust storms in the heartland to the grim shadows cast by skyscrapers onto pitiless city streets. Photography emerged in varying shades of gray, often like storm clouds, ranging from stark to somber, such as Dorothea Lang's images of haunted, migrant faces and the FBI's most-wanted posters. Even Busby Berkeley's screen spectaculars were shot in black and white, lacking a certain dimension in their superficial buoyancy.

But the World's Fair was a never-ending sunburst of color and light and motion and free Coca-Cola.

Deliberately, the fair ignored the past, as well as the families on relief, the sick, the hungry, the abused, societal victims for whom no one claimed an iota of responsibility. The future was all: hope, promise, the bountiful. It promulgated the era's sensation of speed, of streamliners hurtling to anywhere, airplanes soaring into the sun.

I ran across a talking, cigarette-smoking robot, Electro, and his robotic dog Sparko; a doughnut-dunking bar; stands hawking nectarine frappe, crepe suzettes, roast beef sandwiches, and square hamburgers; the parachute jump from Life Saver's—one-minute up, twenty seconds down; elephant rides at Frank Buck's Bring 'Em Back Alive Jungle Land; a sixty-foot egg; the time capsule documenting four centuries of civilization, including a Mickey Mouse watch; a stay-dry, walk-through waterfall; Carrier air conditioning's gigantic igloo; Pedro the Voder, the machine with the human voice.

In the Hall of Music, Gypsy Rose Lee stripped to her ample butt, along with other barely clothed cutie-pies advertising their anatomy at the Amazon Village, Cuban Village, Crystal Palace, Billy Rose's Aquacade, and the Savoy Ballroom. Pasties and g-strings were obligatory, but if some of the equipment slipped, hell, accidents happened. The Fair's inherent dignity may have been gingered up by the bump-and-grind flavor of a carnival midway, but I liked ginger.

I got caught up in it all.

The Savoy Ballroom's pavilion was an outpost of the celebrated Harlem club on Lenox Avenue, sometimes known as "The Temple of the Jitterbug," and home to "The World's Greatest Colored Dancers." Here, at the Fair, a troop of inexhaustible hoofers performed the Lindy Hop, Shag, Suzy-Q, Big Apple, and Shim-Sham—and the most beautiful dancer of them all was a statuesque, ebony queen who called herself

Bathsheba, lithe and loose jointed. Not having seen a woman as enchanting since my time in the Belgian Congo, I immediately struck up an acquaintance with Bathsheba. And made an arrangement.

But then it came time to get serious.

With Diana.

She and I sat on a bench overlooking Fountain Lake, mustard from the hot dogs dribbling into our napkins.

"I was really looking forward to the stuffed artichokes, dollface, but this will do."

"Now what's all this about Nazis, darling?"

"Nothing much. Seems some of the Bund's storm troopers plan to sabotage one of the pavilions."

"Dammit, Tokee, why didn't you tell me?"

"Careless of me."

"When will it happen?"

"Tuesday, after the fair closes for the night."

"And you know all this because…"

"My blabbermouth in the Bund, Heinz Hinrichs, one of the better Nazis—if that's not a contradiction."

"And you don't know which pavilion?"

"Heinz only said it'll be pip-pip and cheerio, old chap."

"I'm disappointed in you, Tokee. He told you exactly which one."

"Huh?"

"The British Pavilion, of course."

Diana was always the smarter of the two of us. And often the most dauntless. Of course, she carried a blowgun with darts garnished by Kyle's venom while I only packed a piece.

I said, "We ought to tell the cops."

"So unlike you, Tokee." She wadded her used napkin and tossed it with precision into a trash can. "Your informant may not be reliable, and if we go to the police, your cover as Rolfe Schenk might be blown. Absolutely not. We'll handle it ourselves."

"But, dollface, the two of us staking out the British Pavilion, late, the fair practically deserted? The building's too big. The Nazis could go to the front or back. The logistics are impossible."

"Vladimir Zworykin will help us. We'll set up his cameras focusing on the pavilion, on all sides, and we'll monitor the images on TRK-12s. When the Nazis come, or if, we'll see them, they won't see us."

"Diana…"

"Don't thank me, Tokee, just raid that arsenal of yours and arm us well. It may take more than my blowgun."

"I'll get to work on it tomorrow, dollface, but tonight I have a surprise for you. Oh, and here she comes now. Diana, meet Bathsheba."

That night, in her penthouse, as Diana and Bathsheba clung to one another, Diana cautioned me.

"You may only look, Tokol. Right now, Bathsheba's all mine."

Kyle and I watched, and while I couldn't get into the head of a king cobra, I guessed we both liked what we saw.

The following morning, back at the Fair, I went into action, enlisting the aid of Electro and his mechanical dog Sparko. Electro was seven feet tall, weighed two-hundred-sixty-five pounds, and while slow on his metallic feet, he wasn't one to mess with. His aluminum carcass concealed a system of photoelectric cells, telephone relays, vacuum tubes, camshafts, gears, and motors—and he reacted to voice commands. Sparko could bark, sit up, beg, and bite.

For his powerful synthesized voice, AT&T's Pedro the

Voder was also deputized. All it took to prompt Pedro to speak was pressing the keys and foot pedals on a typewriter-like console. The Voder could even sing "Auld Lang Syne."

Two buildings made up the British Pavilion, separated by a narrow thoroughfare. In the main building, the Lincoln Cathedral's copy of the Magna Charta was protected in a bulletproof glass case, replicas of the Crown jewels sparkled in the Royal Room, and in the Silver Room the Royal Mint's coins and medals were displayed in metallic magnificence.

But I suspected the Nazis wanted to make a point more than theft.

When Tuesday night came, the cameras in position, Diana, Vlad, and I studied the screens at the RCA Pavilion's bank of receivers. Electro and Sparko were stationed in the rear, hidden motionless in the shadows. The good thing about robots was that they were patient, rarely complained, and never needed to piss. We had also set up a loudspeaker system and Klieg lights, which could be activated remotely.

Vlad first spotted the culprits on the monitors. Five of them dressed in wetsuits, which led me to believe they avoided gate security and infiltrated the fairgrounds by swimming from the Bay through Flushing Creek. Ah, Teutonic ingenuity. As expected, they went directly to the British Pavilion, two going to the rear, the other three remaining in front.

They got right to work, removing obvious explosive materials from their rucksacks.

At the key moment, we switched on the Kliegs, while by loudspeaker I ordered Electro to attack and Sparko to sic 'em. Diana and I, armed with Model 1928A1 45-caliber Thompson submachine guns, converged on the pavilion, firing into the air. Startled by the light and noise and the attack of a giant robot and metallic dog, the Nazis were caught by surprise before they could light a single fuse. Operated by Vlad, the machine with the human voice, Pedro the Voder, boomed, YOU ARE UNDER ARREST. DO NOT MOVE."

As they cowered, hands in the air, the boxheads begged, "Don't shoot, *bitte*, don't shoot."

So much for the master race.

Alerted by the brouhaha, the fair's security guards rushed to the pavilion, taking the Nazis into custody, while Diana and I quietly retreated to the shadows. With the recovery of the bomb-making paraphernalia, there was evidence galore to send the saboteurs up the river.

"Our work here is done," I solemnly proclaimed to Vlad and Diana.

"Oh, shush, Tokee, darling," Diana said as she popped a kiss on my cheek.

But there remained the little matter of Fritz Kuhn.

In addition to everything else, I remained cursed by The Man With Two Faces, so close we had been in both life and death. Not just in the dark when Janus violently tarnished my dreams, but in daylight as I encountered the mundane that reminded me of his sandpaper cheek when he forgot to shave, the embarrassing laugh at inappropriate moments, the bottomless of his voice, and, ultimately, the murderous rage. I had heard it said that a man truly had but one close friend in his entire life. Janus had been that friend—until he marked me for death.

But he could no longer threaten me.

Could he?

Understandably, the German American Bund was disconcerted by the arrests of five of their gunsels. I commiserated with Heinz Hinrichs as we pulled back innumerable ales at Rambacher's Bierstube.

"They were our best storm troopers," Heinz said. "I do not understand how they could have been caught like that."

"Maybe we have a traitor among us."

"*Nein*. A good German is always true to his race."

"At least you weren't with them, Heinz. The Bund can't afford to lose you."

"You are a good *freund*, Rolfe. Unlike Fritz. Him I do not trust."

"You still think Kuhn is stealing from the Bund?"

"I know because as head of security I have access to the Bund's books, and I have seen where he has made fraudulent entries. I happen to know he stole nearly nine-thousand dollars from the rally at Madison Square Garden because I saw the original receipts. But the figures were altered in the books."

"What are you going to do about it?"

"*Nichts*. If I approached him directly he would have me fired and tortured. If I went to the Bund's national officers, who he controls, he would have me fired, tortured, and shot. Dissension within the Bund is not taken lightly."

"I've got a brainstorm, Heinz. Why don't I steal the books and give them to the right person, say Manhattan District Attorney Tom Dewey?"

"The books are kept locked in the safe at Bund headquarters. Except for me, only Kuhn knows the combination."

"Give *me* the combination."

"If I do, Kuhn will know it was me and shoot me."

"Not if he thinks the combination was beaten out of you by, perhaps, a burglar who broke into Bund headquarters and left you tied to a chair. Kuhn may still shoot you, but not because he thought you gave him up."

It was a good plan.

Hinrichs made it known to Kuhn that he would be working late that night on some sort of new security strategy for the Bund's summer encampment.

When Kuhn arrived in the morning, he found Room 5 in disarray, tables and chairs overturned, files strewn about, the safe door open, the ledgers gone, and Heinz gagged and tied to a chair, having been roughed up. As he was untied, Heinz explained that he and a masked burglar had surprised each other, but the intruder, obviously a Jew by the way he said *mazel tov* as he left, got the upper hand. Heinz had made his self-inflicted injuries look good. Too good. A black eye and a cracked cheekbone.

The Bund's books in hand, I made a beeline to the office of Thomas E. Dewey.

Despite his cheesy little mustache, Tom had made a name for himself as a special prosecutor busting the rackets—especially after hitting the jackpot: Lucky Luciano. Riding on a tide of popularity, Dewey moved into the Manhattan Criminal Courts building on Centre Street as district attorney, where he established a team of forensic accountants to investigate financial wrongdoing.

He and I became acquaintances after meeting at a Republican fund raiser, I being a generous GOP contributor despite my New Deal proclivities. In my line, it helped to be accepted within all circles. I even played golf with Archbishop Spellman, who had the good grace to bless me even after I beat his divine ass four under par with two birdies and one eagle.

Dewey was a confirmed New Yorker.

"Tokol," he said, "If you're not in New York you're camping out."

He had political ambitions, having once run for governor, defeated but unbowed. A presidential bid was not out of the question.

It was in Dewey's prosecutorial blood to go after Fritz Kuhn.

As I sat across from him in his office, he said, "Where did you get these financial records, Tokol?"

"They mysteriously arrived on my doorstep, like a baby delivered by a stork."

"I can't use evidence I obtained unlawfully."

"You didn't obtain the evidence unlawfully, Tom. Consider it a gift from a long-legged bird with a thick bill."

Dewey's accountants picked through the Bund's books line by line. Kuhn had failed to report $4,855 on sales of swastikas, armbands, Hitler coffee mugs, and other Bund crap to members, neglected declaring $8,907 from the MSG rally, siphoned off $4,424 from various Bund subsidiaries, plus misappropriating hundreds of dollars for himself and his mistress. All told, the embezzled funds amounted to $14,548.

The grand jury indicted Kuhn, and a bench warrant was issued for his arrest.

I got a frantic call from Heinz.

"Rolfe, Fritz got wind of his indictment. He is downstairs right now loading his car, about to flee the city."

"Stop him."

"If I do, the Bund will know I was colluding against him."

"Then let the air out of his tires. I'll be uptown in twenty minutes."

The traffic was impossible, and my taxi arrived seconds too late.

"He fixed the flat and got away, Tokol," Heinz said. "But you can catch him. Take my Studebaker Champion. He is driving a Ford V-8 sedan, New York license 3Y6974. From the Holland Tunnel he will use Route Twenty-Two to Krumsville,

Pennsylvania."

"Where the hell is that?"

"Twenty miles west of Allentown. The Bund has supporters in the area, and he could hide out there indefinitely."

"But not after they find out he stole Bund funds."

"He will deny it. That it was a setup by Jew-loving Bolsheviks."

"Are you coming with me?"

"I must stay here. It must not appear I had anything to do with this."

Kuhn managed to give me the slip. Apparently suspecting he might be followed, he must have turned off Route 22 to head west in a more circuitous route. I continued on to Krumsville, little more than a crossroad, with a single gas station, café, and motel collectively called Schlenker's. Just in case, I drove well beyond it before turning around and heading back.

I was filling the tank at Schlenker's when a Ford V-8 sedan, New York license 3Y6974, pulled into the lot. Kuhn got out, and went into the café. Through the window I saw him eating *bienestich* and drinking *kaffee*.

I blocked his car with the Studebaker, made a collect call from a payphone to Tom Dewey's detectives, and waited. Encountering me as he left the café, Kuhn gaped in surprise, his tongue seeming about to break from its moorings. But he recovered faster than a fox. Although I was no longer wearing my icky Austrian corporal mustache, he recognized me.

He said, "I would ask what you are doing here, but it is perfectly clear. You must be the traitor who broke into my office, subdued my security chief, and stole our financial ledgers. Is your name really Rolfe Schenk?"

"I'm any name you'd like to call me, Fritz, and I'm sure

you have a lot of them."

"Very funny, Mr. Schenk. You slay me—as you Americans say."

"That's exactly what I want to talk to you about."

"I will wager you are not even German."

"They wouldn't let me join the master race."

"No doubt you have sheeny blood. Those who are not of a sound genealogy in this world are mere chaff. All human culture—art, science, technology—are almost exclusively the creative product of the Aryan."

"Somebody should have told that to Einstein. Speaking of creative product, didn't you know you were indicted by a grand jury in Manhattan?"

"I had no idea."

"What are you doing in this dump instead of, say, standing before a judge for your arraignment?"

"I, I am just passing through. I was headed to a Bund rally in Chicago, and I am about to open a Bund youth camp in Milwaukee. You cannot keep me here against my will. You have no authority, whoever you are, obviously not the police. And driving a Studebaker Champion, which looks like the one owned by Heinz Hinrichs."

"Yeah, I jacked it. Heinz will be mighty pissed when he finds out it's gone. He's probably still hurting from the whacking I gave him in your office."

"Stand aside. I will leave now."

I patted the convincer under my coat.

"Why don't the two of us stay here and keep each other company until the gumshoes from Tom Dewey's office get here from Manhattan."

He spat. "Tom Dewey. And how is your friend Tom Dewey? Do not tell me. He is probably drinking gin with Walter

Winchell at the Stork Club."

"I'll say hi to both of them for you the next time I'm in the Cub Room, which will be just as soon as I return to civilization. In the meantime let's put on our lederhosen and sing a few rounds of 'The Hofbräuhaus Song.'"

"You give me a pain in my belly."

"Really? Maybe my voodoo doll is working after all."

Kuhn pointed to a bench near the entrance to the café.

"Since we may have a long wait, perhaps we may sit over there?"

"Good idea, Fritz, I'd like to take the load off. Feels like I've been driving all day."

We sat. Kuhn, his head bobbing, appeared to doze off. I felt like nodding myself, and tried to resist. But, damn, I was bushed and, well, I conked out. But only for a moment, I swear, long enough, however, not to feel Fritz reaching into my pocket to extract the keys to Heinz's Studebaker, which was still blocking Kuhn's car.

But I came alert as soon as I heard the Studebaker start up.

Sonofabitch!

As the car began to back up, I leaped from the bench to the car's rear end, as if I could halt it like Superman. Instead, the back fender on the passenger's side bumped me, knocking me on my ass. Kuhn braked the car, turned it, then drove straight at me. I rolled to safety just inches from the wheels as it roared past.

Kuhn had the keys but not my trusty Smith and Wesson, which I whipped out, firing from a prone position through a plume of dust at the escaping car. One of the bullets caught the back tire on the driver's side, and the Studebaker swerved out of control, leaving the road, and smashed into a white oak.

When I caught up to Kuhn, he was hunched over the steering wheel, visibly shaken but otherwise appearing to be okay. I opened the door, grabbed him by the collar, and dragged him to the ground.

"Nazi prick," I said, "you almost killed me."

"*Alles hat ein Ende, nur die Wurst hat zwei*," he replied, which I took to mean, "Everything has an end, only the sausage has two."

Lucky for him that Dewey's dicks arrived in time to take the Nazi loser off my hands. I had been about to inflict a beating that would impress even Kuhn's hallowed Führer.

Kuhn's trial was a circus. His lawyer maintained that as Bund Fuehrer, he had the absolute right to squander the group's money, even flushing it down the toilet if he chose. Love letters—*to you my golden angel, I kiss your hands and everything*—written by the married Kuhn to his paramour were introduced to show how he used Bund funds to bankroll his affair. Dewey and LaGuardia were called as witnesses by Kuhn's lawyer, who claimed his client was being tried only because of their animus.

Isadore Greenbaum, Diana, and I watched as the jury, after eight and a half hours, returned its verdict: guilty of five counts of grand larceny and forgery.

Kuhn, stoic like a good German, was led to the Tombs to await sentencing as Greenbaum put his hand on my shoulder.

"Tokol, when I headed the committee from the National Jewish Council to ask you to obliterate Fritz Kuhn, I wasn't sure you could pull it off. But you exceeded our expectations."

"I had a great friend once, Isadore. Clarence Darrow. He told me that true patriotism hates injustice in its own land, and here we saw the Nazis at work in America. I had no choice."

Judge James Wallace gave Kuhn five years in Dannemora.

The German American Bund went into decline after its most visible leader was put under lock and key. Even Americans of German stock could smell the odor of evil.

Heinz Hinrichs made the wise decision to resign from the Bund.

We met one last time at Schweinsteiger's Rathskeller for a farewell drink or more.

He said, "I guess I cannot call you Rolfe anymore, so whoever you are, every German in America owes you a measure of gratitude for bringing down a bad man."

"All Nazis are bad, Heinz, so you were right to quit the Bund."

"I even forgive you for wrecking my Studebaker."

"Technically, Kuhn did it. So the Bund will have to reimburse you."

"They won't. Another reason I am leaving."

"To where?"

"I am taking a job as a mechanical engineer at Grumman Aerospace in Bethpage."

"Hmmm."

"What is the matter? Does that disturb you?"

"It's just that... You might be privy to vital aeronautics information of possible interest to the Nazis."

"Quite right. *Skoal*, if you will pardon my Viking."

The World's Fair was about to wrap up its first season, so Diana and I celebrated at Le Restaurant du Pavilion de France. We toasted the fair, we toasted New York, we toasted ourselves. Yet a shadow hung over us with the world in violence and turmoil.

As our defense plants worked overtime to fulfill military contracts, the Great Depression slowly ran out of steam. Just like the World's Fair itself, which was hemorrhaging so much dough it was hard to believe it could sustain another season.

After our coquilles Saint Jacques, poached turbot, and stuffed artichokes, Diana eyed me quizzically over coffee.

"There's something on your mind, Tokee. I can always tell when something's not copacetic."

I sighed. "I wasn't sure how you'd take it, dollface, but I'm thinking about enlisting."

"I'm a big girl, even though for us it's always been two for the price of one. The French Foreign Legion again?"

"There's word going around that Wild Bill Donovan, a chum of mine, is in Europe to see how America can help our allies. It's all hush hush. Spy stuff amuses me. I just might go to North Africa on my own, see if I can scare up some trouble on behalf of our friends. Casablanca, maybe. Or Algiers. I know people there."

"And what about us, Tokee, darling? Where do I stand in all this?"

"With me, I hope."

We locked lips.

Good evening, Mr. and Mrs. America and all the ships at sea. Let's go to press.

Flash! A personal note. Nineteen thirty-nine brings a special decade to a close. With another war underway in Europe nothing will be the same. It's been the age of speed and light; geometrically scored skyscrapers; Gershwin and Copland; Gable and Lombard; saxophone and Theremin; Fred and Ginger; Twentieth Century Limited and Caribbean Clipper; Busby Berkeley and Jean Harlow; Pretty Boy Floyd and Machine Gun Kelly; Speedsters and Roadsters; Bakelite babble from Atlantic to Pacific—all tempered by depression, breadlines, dustbowls, and the rattle of tommy guns. Auf Wiedersehen, my late friend.

Flash! Your intrepid reporter has learned exclusively that his Certain Acquaintance is no longer in the States, but is overseas bravely doing his part to help our allies in their struggle against the Axis enemy. C.A. is not waiting for the war to come to our shores. Just where he is cannot be revealed, but you can be certain that at the right time the Nazis will feel his fury.

...For Jergens Lotion, this is Walter Winchell wishing you lotions of love.

seven

Operation Torch 1940

My hovel in an unnamed alley of the Casbah was rank with
the stench of something dead plus the odor of piss infiltrating
through the slat serving as the lone window. I was under the
command of a brigade of cockroaches, who became so familiar I gave them names: lieutenant, sergeant, corporal. Down
the hall stood a yellowed sink with a leaky faucet, while the
toilet was a hole in a listing wooden cubicle outdoors. Admit-
tedly, it wasn't as ritzy as my room at the Y in New York, but
it would do.

Yet in my anonymity I almost preferred these sorrowful
digs—a mere handful of francs each week, a dollar or two—
over the luxurious Le Saint George Hotel, home away from
home to potentates, diplomats, and celebrities from Churchill
to Piaf to de Beauvoir to Chaplin, even Bogart.

Word circulated that Bogie was in Algiers with director
John Huston scouting locations for a new film, although no
one had actually seen the two—at least not without a drink in
their mitts.

What was I doing in Algeria living in such mean accommodations?

Serving my nation against the Axis menace.

The Nazis would murder me if they knew who I was and
why I was there. God knew the city was alive with spies, including spooks of our own.

Whenever I left my cell, I darkened my skin to a subtle olive and dressed in traditional native garb. Burnoose, fez, and sandals. The burnoose had sufficient folds in which to secret my gat. I spoke French, Arabic, and a bit of Berber, but primarily I conducted myself like a drooling moron, so people gave me a wide birth.

When the call for salah arrived five times a day, wherever I was I obediently prostrated myself in the name of Allah, the Most Beneficent, Owner of the Universe, Guardian of the Faith, the All-Aware—even though supplicants earned additional credits for actually worshiping *inside* a mosque. Indeed, the Djama'a al-Kebir Mosque, built in the year 1097, was on Rue de la Marine, a mere five-minute walk from my hole.

The streets of Algiers vividly evoked a coexisting cultural mélange: fashionably dressed Westerners sipping the local brew in outdoor cafes, old men in fezzes playing dominoes on makeshift tables, Muslim women in black niqabs.

I had been in Manhattan in my Chrysler Building office when I got the call from Wild Bill Donovan to join him in Algiers to discuss something vital. The flamboyant Donovan was a hero of the Great War, wounded three times, and a conservative Republican who eight years ago had run unsuccessfully for governor of New York. Although an FDR liberal, I contributed to Donovan's failed campaign because in my racket it was prudent to cull friendships from all political spectrums.

Bill's transatlantic phone line from London was staticky.

"Tokol, I'm fully aware of your various clandestine activities, so I've arranged for you to take a military charter to Algiers. You've been booked into a hotel under the name Stephen P. Swan, a salesman of valves for oil and gas pipelines. I can't reveal more on the phone. I'll be leaving England for Algeria tomorrow."

"Is it safe for you to fly out of London right now?" I asked.

"Some little war's not going to stop me."

Little war my derriere. Hitler's offensive in France had just forced more than three-hundred thousand British soldiers to flee Dunkirk in every skiff, sailboat, yacht, trawler, ferry, tugboat, and garbage scow they could commandeer. A humiliating defeat, but a logistical miracle. London was now under siege from the air.

"Tokol, let me remind you this is all on the QT, and you know what that means."

Even as Europe was cursed by war, the U.S. was officially neutral.

Diana took it in stride when I told her I was flying the next day on a military transport out of Mitchel Army Airfield in Hempstead Plains.

"Guess I won't be seeing you for a while, Tokee, darling," she said. "I'll be lonely."

"You've got Kyle."

"He's been a bit crotchety, so we're not speaking right now. Don't suppose you'll tell me where you're going."

I kissed her on the lips as if to seal our silence.

"Maybe I'll be able to send for you," I said vaguely.

"I won't hold my breath."

"Anyway, you've got plenty to do on the home front."

"I may go to England to help wrap bandages."

The military had designated Mitchel Field as the U.S. Air Defense Command. From there I hitched a flight on an Army Curtiss C-46 Commando, holding tight to a bench on the upper passenger level for the bumpy, unheated Trans-Atlantic crossing. My fellow passengers were a surly bunch who spent the flight drinking stale thermos coffee and smoking. They didn't ask where I was going and I reciprocated.

We refueled in Gander, Dublin, and Madrid before landing at Maison Blanche Airport in Algiers.

The plane skirted much of the European coast, of course. France had fallen to the Jerries, who occupied the north, while the Nazi-puppet Pétain controlled the south, the colonies, and what was left of the French military. The Vichy wasted no time in passing the *Statut des Juifs*, and Algerian Jews were stripped of their citizenship overnight. Jewish internment camps were set up at Bedeau and Djelfa.

At the airport, I was met by Donovan's limo, whose driver supplied me with an appropriately constructed passport with my new name and photo, and ferried me to the Hotel Saint George on Rue Michelet.

It was a searingly hot day, and Algiers appeared whitewashed under the sun, the low-slung houses, narrow streets, hermitic courtyards, arches, and minarets, a sprawl against the Mediterranean, an almost unnatural blue. I was no stranger here, a visitor many times during my Foreign Legion days, and where I honed my French.

It was also where I first met Gazala Lazaar, a young woman with whom I had, one might say, an arrangement. I wondered if she was still in the city and if I dared look her up. No. It would wreck my cover.

Still…

The mosaic-lined hotel, once an Ottoman palace, boasted gardens of roses and jasmine, sheltered by palm and banana trees, and in the distance the Bay of Algiers. After I checked in, my single bag was dispatched to my room while I was escorted to the suite of William J. Donovan, a cut-glass Irishman from Buffalo who traveled far and lived well.

We clinked our glasses of single-malt Glenfiddich.

"To our arriving safely in Algiers," I said.

"Almost didn't make it, Tokol. My plane strayed over the Channel Islands, and came under antiaircraft fire. But I was worried not. If I survived being shot down and captured by the Krauts a potassium cyanide capsule would have been between my teeth before they knew it."

Donovan wasn't called Wild Bill for naught. His combat exploits earned him the Medal of Honor, Légion d'Honneur, Order of the British Empire, Croce di Guerra, Order of Leopold, Order of Polonia Restituta, and Croix de Guerre with Palm and Silver Star.

"Tokol, FDR and I don't agree politically—except regarding the Nazis. He asked me to observe British intelligence first hand, and a Canadian agent, code-named Intrepid, introduced me to MI6 operations overseas. I now run the COI, Coordinator of Information, which is consolidating all U.S. intelligence."

"Bill, it's become perfectly clear. You want me to be a spy."

"Not just any spy, Tokol. You're here because of Operation Torch."

"Never heard of it."

"Code for the American invasion of West Africa."

"We're officially neutral."

"We'll be in the damned war as sure as Glenfiddich is as smooth as a baby's butt. Soon, Egypt will be overrun by the Wehrmacht, which thinks it can save the asses of their little Italian pets. Within two years we'll invade Morocco and Algeria and bash the bastards point-blank."

"The Vichy military might have something to say about that, Bill. The French think West Africa's their gift from God."

"Three days after our invasion, the Vichy will be kissing

our boots—and you can take that to Chase National Bank. Why the hell are the French in Africa to begin with? I don't recall Algeria inviting them. I've already set up a clandestine unit in Algiers to begin intelligence as part of Operation Torch."

"Bill, I want to do my part but I don't think my sitting in an office—"

"Not an office, Tokol. I want you in the field. Algiers is teeming with Nazis and their collaborators, so for us it's perfect. We've already set you up as a valve salesman, which will get you in to meet the right people in Fascist circles. I warn you, however, it'll be dangerous, and I don't want your corpse discovered in some fetid alley in the Casbah."

"What if I could squeeze even closer, such as actually infiltrating the Nazis' Algerian ministry? Maybe posing as a harmless, unskilled native."

"Fine. Dump their guano. Pick up their trash. But paw through it for pearls first."

"Who do I report to?"

"A young man I've put in charge of our Algerian operations. Henry Hyde. Cambridge, Harvard Law. Speaks French, German. Married to the daughter of a French baron. He's acquiring maps, measuring the coastline, charting fields, watching ship movements, and getting messages in and out by shortwave. Ain't no Mickey Mouse operation."

"When do I start?"

"Yesterday."

I left Donovan to formulate my plans. First, I would keep my room at the Saint George in my guise as Stephen P. Swan of Dallas, Texas, purveyor of valves, which I familiarized myself with by reading the voluminous research Donovan's team supplied. Second, I planned an additional identity as Salaah al-Abdoo, common laborer, illiterate, and devoted follower of Mohammed, praised messenger of Allah and Keeper of All Statistics.

Should be fun. Too bad Diana wasn't here to join in.

Late in the afternoon, I wandered the streets to refresh my recollection of a city so French that Africa almost seemed an afterthought.

On Rue Crémieux near the university, I slid into a chair at an outdoor café. The adjoining table was occupied by two French-speaking men, one young, the other older, drinking coffee, smoking, and talking relentlessly. From their conversation, it was apparent the occasion was a farewell to the younger man, slender with a high forehead. While it was impossible not to overhear them, I took cover behind a copy of *Le Quotidien d'Algérie*.

The older said, "So, Albert, what are your plans after you cross the Mediterranean?"

"I've arranged to work as a reporter at *Paris-Soir*, which relocated to Lyon due to the occupation. Don't look at me like that, Jean. A job under the Vichy regime in France, is better than no job at all in Algiers."

"Vichy is a place of sulfurous waters, mud baths, and colonic irrigation, falsely guaranteed to cure gout, liver disease, and rheumatism."

"To be practical, it takes a certain amount of income to live no matter where one is, and having money is a way of being free of money."

"Do you suppose you'll ever return to the *Alger Républicain*?"

"A newspaper run by communists and anarchists in Algeria? It was doomed. First they censored us, then they confiscated our paper stock, and finally we were banned. But we were defiant. Thinking people are not obligated to be on the side of their executioners."

"Albert, you're basically a rebel."

"What's a rebel? Merely a man who says no. I exist as long as I rebel."

"How's your novel coming, the one about that *Pied-Noir* murdering for no good reason an Arab on the beach at Oran?"

"Slowly, Jean. But I disagree when you say the Arab was murdered for no good reason. A novel is philosophy put into images, and a work that will last must consist of profound ideas. In other words, fiction is the lie through which we tell the truth."

"Was the Arab's murder a crime of passion or logic?"

"The boundary between the two is rarely clear." He stubbed out his cigarette butt with the toe of his shoe. "But for me, there's no passion without a struggle. We're all capable of good deeds, Jean. However, if a man hasn't passion, he leaves me cold."

The young man drained his coffee and stood.

"I must say *adieu*. But I've been asking myself a question for which you might have the answer." A pause. "Should I kill myself or have another cup of coffee?"

There was an uncomfortable silence for a moment, then both laughed. The voyager left after an exchange of hugs and kisses.

It occurred to me that Operation Torch might find value in a youthful anti-Fascist stationed among the Vichy in Lyon, particularly one who could so cavalierly balance life on one hand with a cup of coffee on the other. I made a mental note for Hyde.

Leaning over, I said to Jean, who remained at his table, "I couldn't help overhearing your conversation, *monsieur*. Your friend seems to have an extraordinary mind."

"*Oui.* I was once his teacher. He's a genius, although he says he has enough problems just being a man."

"What's his name?"

"Albert Camus."

My next step was to snoop around the German consulate on Rue des Laperlier, an imposing building topped by a Nazi flag and patrolled by churlish sentries. In my shabby Algerian garb, I knew I'd be curtly rebuffed at the front gate, so I reconnoitered to the loosely guarded rear where I easily breached the wall and found my way to the trash cans. I busied myself poking through the garbage.

Suddenly I heard him demanding an explanation from me. "*Was machst du denn hier, schweinhund?*"

It was a private in a Waffen-SS uniform, aiming his Karabiner 98k at my heart. I threw my hands up, shaking my head as if I didn't understand why he was demanding to know the reason for my defiling presence.

"*Sprechen sie Deutsch?*" he snarled.

Wildly gesticulating, I appealed to him in hopeless ignorance.

Finally, in a barely intelligible amalgam of French, Arabic, and English, the two of us communicated awkwardly.

I whined, "No offense, effendi, I was merely cleaning your garbage pails."

Effendi wasn't quite the word to apply in Algeria, but I figured a member of the master race would consider the term agreeably subservient, so I obliged.

"I should shoot you for trespassing on German soil, you piece of Algerian filth."

"Please, effendi, I was trying to help. My services are yours for next to nothing. I will pick your grass with my bare hands, lick the garbage pails clean with my tongue, empty your slops. Perform all that you ask of this poor, humble scullion."

"Get the hell out of here before I shove my boot up your ass. *Schnell!*"

"Yes, effendi. Certainly, effendi. All that you say, effendi."

I backed away bowing, scraping like the miserable piece of bilge I made myself out to be.

"Halt, fuckface. What's your name?"

"I am Salaah al-Abdoo, effendi."

"Where do you live?"

"The Casbah near the mosque, effendi."

He flipped me a coin.

"Go out and buy me a pack of Atikah *cigaretten*, and if you ain't back in ten minutes I'll come looking for you and there'll be hell to pay. And use the front gate from now on."

"Indeed, effendi. Anything you ask of me, effendi. Allah has commanded me to serve."

And so I entered into a private arrangement with Private Otto Glockner, who unwittingly became my entrée to the German Consulate. As his personal servant, serf, drudge, minion, and all-around whipping boy, I shined his boots, cleaned his rifle, brought him schnapps, and, above all, while he loafed gave him a heads up whenever his sergeant came prowling around. Glockner paid me the equivalent of pennies a day, and soon my duties expanded.

Thus, I was a common sight as I weeded, mowed, cleaned, lugged, toiled, and rifled the garbage for scraps of intelligence, some potentially useful. To the casual observer, I was a common-as-dirt servant, seen yet not seen, rather like my Zulu namesake, the mythological tokoloshe, who became invisible simply by ingesting H_2O. The Krauts allowed me the run of the consulate grounds, and I was even able to enter the kitchen, sometimes thrown scraps of wiener schnitzel and bratwurst.

The best part was that no one knew I spoke German, so they blabbed freely around me.

Glockner, who regarded me as an object of his amusement, made a point of kicking my ass on a daily basis, sometimes hourly. In the military, a private was the lowest of the low, but Glockner boasted something even lower. Me. To toady up to his sergeant, a brute named Fiedler, Otto began sharing me with him.

One day as I polished their boots, I listened to them prattling, oblivious of my worthless presence.

"Sarge, when are we getting out of this shithole?" Glockner asked Fiedler. "This ain't no place for Waffen-SS. Why are we even here? We're like security guards. It's time we got back to our original division saw some action."

"You're about to get your wish, private, but if you say a fucking word to anyone I'll see to it you'll be eating *scheisse* the rest of your lousy military career. I ain't supposed to know this, but I do my own poking around in the colonel's office while he's out getting laid. Rommel's assembling an Afrika Korps, and our unit is joining a Panzer division to bail out the guineas. We're about to ship out to Cyrenaica as part of a big, new offensive in February against the Brits."

"Where the hell is Cyrenaica?"

"You better start boning up on Libya, you *flachwichser*."

Word of an impending offensive in North Africa was worth gold to the Allies. Rommel's planned intervention in Libya may have been ominous, but identifying his ETA was why God made spies.

Hyde, my contact, and I arranged cloak-and-dagger meetings on a palm-shaded bench near a fountain in Le Jardin d'Essai du Hamma in the Mohamed Belouizdad district, and this was one of the best pieces of intel I was able to give him.

I was almost going to miss not having Otto Glockner to kick me around anymore.

Meanwhile, in my pose as Stephen P. Swan of Nemosys Technologies of Dallas—offices in Tulsa and Baton Rouge—I made an appointment to see Félix Brosseau, chief executive officer of Travers Poissonnier, Ltd., an oil and gas consortium.

Brosseau was a *Pied-Noir*, by inclination more French than Algerian, but he spoke unblemished English, the result of four years at MIT.

"Do you know Boston, Mr. Swan?"

"Like the back of my hand. I could write the book on Roxbury."

Boston was an old stomping ground, and I once worked in Dorchester with a pair of IRA gunrunners, nice guys actually, although a little too fond of their Guinness.

Brosseau happened to be a Red Sox fan. This led to a rigorous debate regarding the BoSox versus the Yanks, although my heart was secretly with the Wichita Oilers, 1930 Western League champs—until they defected to Muskogee.

Then we got down to business.

"Word travels fast, Mr. Swan. How did you learn about our natural gas strike in Hassi R'Mel? I didn't know the news had reached America."

"When you come right down to it, the oil and gas industry is clannish, and there aren't a lot of secrets. Nemosys Technologies gets in on the ground floor wherever pipelines and valves are needed."

I gave him my pitch, even though Nemosys existed only on paper and a dummy phone line, ostensibly to Dallas, but actually maintained discreetly by the gals at Mrs. Prunella

Mayhem's Accurate Answering Service.

"Nemosys manufactures a complete line of high- and low-pressure valves such as balls, plugs, butterflies, and gates." Blah, blah, blah. "Depending on the hydrocarbon product and pressure requirements, our products are an excellent choice to route high pressure natural gas." Blah, blah, blah. "We recommend expanding gate-type actuators for mainline pipeline block valves and top/bottom support ball valves in compressor stations." Blah, blah, blah."

It sounded like I knew what the hell I was talking about, and Brosseau seemed to be impressed.

"Mr. Swan, we believe there are petroleum assets in the Sahara just waiting to be tapped, though no doubt the war will slow development."

"Have any other, ah, parties shown interest in your find at Hassi R'Mel?"

"As a matter of fact, we've been approached by a representative of Siverdt Trossingen Systems of Munich, Germany. A Herr Matts."

Bingo.

Another score for Hyde.

Félix Brosseau invited me to a reception in the Abd al-Qadir Room of the Saint George, where I met any number of Germans including the consul, the Wehrmacht military attaché, a banker from Stuttgart, and Jan Matts, the man from Siverdt Trossingen.

I wasted no time in talking them up.

"America is officially nonaligned," I assured them, "and the our Congress has passed no fewer than four neutrality acts. President Roosevelt guarantees that Americans will never fight on European soil. Pigs will fly before that happens."

Everyone knew it was a lie, and that the pigs would fly

sooner than later. But all went along with the charade.

I slipped to the bar to replenish my gin rickey as Berber musicians performing taghanimt, nafir, ginbri, and tabl entertained with native songs and dances.

I felt a tap on my shoulder.

"Tokol?" A woman's voice.

Turning, I saw Gazala Lazaar, whom I had known in Algiers in, shall I say, a variety of ways—pre-Diana. She was wearing a stunning karakou with a velvet jacket embroidered with gold threads and sequins, and a long skirt trimmed with lace. Gazala had lost neither her youth nor her penchant for traditional Algerian attire.

"I'm afraid you're mistaken, ma'am. My name's Stephen P. Swan from Dallas, Texas. Married, two daughters."

"I'd know you anywhere, Tokol, even though it's been years. Don't you remember me? Gazala. Those nights we spent on Rue de l'Abreuvoir in the Third District? I still live there on the same floor with the same, romantic view."

"Miss Gazala, I assure you—"

"Lazaar. Gazala's my first name. But you know that, Tokol, don't you?"

"Ma'am, I'm in Algiers on business. I've never been in this city before."

"I'd recognize your face with my eyes closed. You're hard to forget."

"Lots of people look alike, Miss Lazaar."

"Tokol, the baby wasn't yours."

"I have no idea what you're talking about, ma'am. Please excuse me..."

"We need to speak."

"You're mistaken."

"Tokol, I can't believe that I—"

"I must go, ma'am."

"Are you staying here at the Saint George?"

"Sorry."

Awkwardly, I managed to shrink from the crowded room, presumably unobserved. Damn. Gazala nearly compromised me. She was as enticing as ever, but I'd need to go out of my way to avoid her in the future.

Did she say baby?

Gazala aside, I forged ahead, wining and dining my new acquaintances, the most accessible being Jan Matts of Siverdt Trossingen Oil, ostensibly a friendly competitor. For a German, he proved to be a decent boozing companion, a consummate fan of Marlene Dietrich, the films of Ernst Lubitsch, Lotte Lenya singing Kurt Weill, and the guitar of Django Reinhardt. But best was finding out from Matts about a new German pipeline under construction in Tobruk.

Mornings, afternoons, and sometimes at night, I performed my usual scullery duties at the Nazi Consulate, accepting Private Glockner's abuse with a humility worthy of Gandhi. Then the fateful day came when Otto confronted me near the ash heap.

"al-Abdoo, you butthole, get over here. I got news for you."

"Indeed, effendi, anything, effendi."

"You're out of here as of right now. Our detachment of Waffen SS, which shouldn't be here in the first place, ships out in the morning, and the consulate don't want you around no more—or any other of your kind."

"But, effendi, surely…"

"So scram the fuck out. You stick your camel snoot in here again and you'll be shot on sight. But, say, I'll drink a stein in your honor tonight when me and my pals celebrate our leaving. Now, *schnell*, you sand monkey."

I was sacked. Just like that after weeks of gathering worthy intel while enduring Glockner's pitiless indignities. But all was not lost. Since I was now persona non grata at the consulate, I decided to give Otto a farewell gift.

What the hell did I have to lose now?

He and his pals gathered for a farewell fete at Brauhaus Veronika on Place Bugeaud, the only German café in Algiers. Through the front window I, dressed in my usual peasant duds, watched them ingurgitating thirstily while singing off-key their German drinking songs. *Weißt nicht wie gut ich dir bin / Ja, ja, ja, ja, weißt nicht wie gut ich dir bin*. Fortuitously, as I was plotting how to separate Glockner from his chums, he emerged to take a piss in the empty alley.

"*Achtung!*" I shouted, before he had a chance to button his fly.

His shoulders stiffened in the Pavlovian way of all good Germans. One thing about the Krauts, rarely was there an order they didn't obey.

"Glockner, *ihre Schubladen fallen. Schnell!*"

He was about to comply and drop his drawers, but stopped when he observed me in the shadows, my face only partially hidden, by design.

"al-Abdoo," he said, "is that you, you damned camel jacker?"

"Do as I say, private."

"Naw, can't be al-Abdoo. He's a stupid, ignorant raghead that don't speak no German."

"*Nein, dummkopf.*"

I withdrew a seventeenth-century, single-edge nimcha from the scabbard affixed to my waist, and flourished it like a corsair. It was a gorgeous twenty-one inch saber of fine steel engraved with sun, moon, and stars, with a hilt composed of tortoiseshell and mother of pearl. Instead of merely slicing through the belt of Private Glockner, as it managed in a flash, the sword properly belonged to a museum of antiquities. In fact, it did. Borrowed precisely for this ceremonial occasion from the Musée National des Antiquités on Boulevard Krim Belkacem.

"What the hell?" Glockner said, with his trousers bunched down around his ankles.

"Now your tunic, Otto."

"You can't make me—"

Woosh, went the sword as it slashed through the upper layer of his clothes. He tried to run, but with the trousers enclosing his shoes he tripped, pitched forward, and fell face down on the piss-soaked cobblestones. His fat ass was such a tantalizing target, I couldn't help but jab him in the rear, just enough to make it count.

"Eeyow," he cried. "Don't you know I'm a member of the Waffen—"

I interrupted him with a number of healthy thwacks with the flat side of the blade, and a few more pricks in the shape of a swastika, just for fun, enough to bring a little decorative blood to the surface.

"Why are you doing this?" Glockner moaned, then began bawling like a *kleinkind*.

"You're a fine example of the master race, Otto. If Sergeant Fiedler only could see you... Hmmm. Maybe he will."

I was tempted to send Glockner to wherever Nazis went when they left this sphere, one less Heinie to whack on the battlefield, but it was too easy so I spared him.

"Stand up, Otto. Make sure everything's off. Every stitch. Yeah, shoes and socks too."

At nimcha point, I marched him, naked, bleeding, sniveling, and humiliated to the busy street, paraded him around a bit, then prodded him back into the restaurant, where the sight of his reeking chassis brought a halt to the rambunctious drinking ditty his buddies were singing.

"So *lange, sauger*," I called, as I disappeared into the sidewalk crowds.

Looking back, I saw Glockner's pals led by Sergeant Fiedler pour from the restaurant into the street looking for me, but I was way ahead of them.

As I returned to the Casbah, I observed Humphrey Bogart and John Huston drunkenly weaving out of a saloon on Rue d'Isly. I'd never run into Bogie, but I knew John through his father Walter. I first met Walter backstage after a performance of Weill's *Knickerbocker Holiday* at the Barrymore in which he played Peter Stuyvesant. Son John proved to be a real hell raiser.

But I didn't dare identity myself, particularly in peasant garb and carrying a sword.

I heard John say, "I don't give a damn what you claim, Bogie. God's not dead, he's drunk."

"Yeah, me too. I never should have switched from scotch to martinis."

"Say, I forget. Where are we? Algiers or Casablanca?"

"I dunno. It's all Africa, isn't it?"

The Casbah sprawled mazelike on a hillside sloping toward the Mediterranean, since the sixteenth century an unfathomable jungle of earthen brick, stucco, stone, and wooden abodes, punctuated by the occasional telephone or electric wire, quarters for tens of thousands of Muslims. The rooftops and terraces constituted a second precinct, where people lived, died, worshipped, mated, built their fires, and hung their laundry.

After my morning ablutions, I left my cave to walk the twisting alleys to the tiny shop where I regularly stood drinking coffee with the thickness of mud and eating almond cakes drenched in honey. I heard a clamor from outside, and when I peeked out I saw gendarmes and uniformed Nazis swaggering arrogantly, shoving people around in the narrow street, congested with vendors, shoppers, loafers, tadghtita pipers, beggars, even a few souls with real places to go.

"Do you know what's going on?" I asked the sullen shopkeeper.

"The *Sûreté Nationale* likes to bully us while posturing for the Nazis."

"Any reason in particular?"

"Seems some *béni-oui-oui* thrashed a German enlisted man last night in an alley on Place Bugeaud. The *gendarmerie* were here before dawn searching for the bugger. They've put up a reward and wanted posters." He looked at me suspiciously. "Say, the sketch of the hooligan in the poster looks a lot like, well, you. Indeed, very, very *much* like you."

I had thought I looked a lot like nobody, and now I was a *béni-oui-oui*, a Muslim collaborator with the colonials.

He said, "Humble people like us in the Casbah do not need trouble with the Germans or the French."

I threw down a couple of coins to pay for my coffee and cake.

I was beginning to believe the Casbah was no longer safe for me.

Eluding the gendarmes, I switched to my other guise and returned to my room at the Hotel Saint George, only to find that someone had broken in. The place was a shambles, my bag rifled, papers strewn about, the mattress slashed open. It was not a simple burglary. Whoever got in was looking for something, although I had left nothing revealing, only my Hart Schaffner & Marx suit, labels removed, in the closet.

Clearly, I had been found out.

But by whom?

I met Hyde at our usual bench in Le Jardin d'Essai du Hamma.

Under the shade of the date palms, he said, "The information you've given us has been first rate, Tokol, and we've even been in touch with that young Camus fellow in Lyon. But clearly you've been compromised. And your intemperate attack on some Nazi private in an alley on Place Bugeaud last night didn't help."

"It wasn't intemperate, Henry. They booted me out of the consulate, so effectively my work there was done. I couldn't go back. Besides, the Kraut had it coming."

"Clearly, your cover as a Dallas businessman has been prejudiced as well."

"That's a different story. Someone gave me away."

"Any suspicions?"

"It might have been a German pipeline guy I met at a reception at the Saint George, Jan Matts. Since we're both interested in Travers Poissonnier's business, the break-in could have had something to do with that. Then again it could be Félix Brosseau himself. He studied in America. Still…"

"A good spy suspects everyone."

"Maybe I got too close."

"Tokol, it's obvious your usefulness here has come to an end, and it's no longer safe for you."

"You're kicking me out."

"For your own good. I've been in touch by shortwave with your fiancée, Miss Dryad, and she's waiting for you in London. A Navy Boeing 314 Clipper will fly you from Algiers, so you need to report to the pier at dawn tomorrow. Until then you should remain in your hotel room. We'll post a man outside."

"Forget the protection, Henry. There's someone I have to see. If she agrees."

"I can't guarantee your safety."

"If you can't, who can?"

"Precisely."

Back at the hotel, I phoned Gazala Lazaar.

"Somehow I knew you'd call, Tokol."

"I think I should explain myself before I leave."

"Yes, you should."

"Shall we meet at your place?"

"That wouldn't be a good idea right now. I have certain, ah, commitments. Do you know the Hayreddin Barbarossa Hotel on Rue de Constantine?"

"Yes, it's across from the park."

"I'll meet you there at three in the garden café."

Despite Hyde's fears, I was my usual cautious self. If the Nazis had my number, no doubt they'd try to trail me, which might compromise Gazala, and God knew I'd pained her enough. But I had lots of experience giving bad guys the shake, and in this instance I rode in no fewer than three hacks taking an excursive route. Regardless of the heat, I wore my worsted with my roscoe strapped in an ankle holster.

Despite a name dating to antiquity, the Hayreddin Barbarossa was a colonial hotel with the usual French touches. Its garden, visible from the street, was shaded by palms and cork oak, and adorned with lavender, malope, and paperwhite. Gazala, looking elegant in a cloche hat, sat alone at a table smoking a cigarette in a long holder. Only a few other tables were occupied, mostly by women of a certain age. It appeared safe.

I glided into the chair across the table from her.

"You're late. Just like the Tokol I remember."

She smiled, but it was impossible to tell if the expression was genuine or not. Gazala was sometimes inscrutable.

I said, "A lot has preoccupied me."

"Apparently so, enough to prompt you to lie to me."

"My business here has required a degree of anonymity."

"What's new about that, Tokol? You've always been secretive. In those early days following our first meeting, after you left the Legion, I had no idea where you were half the time. You acquired an unpleasant knack of disappearing for long periods, and then returning unexpectedly, just as you did this time. So I can't say I was surprised."

"A man in my work…"

"Just what is your work, Tokol?"

"You know I can't talk about it."

"It was diamonds once, correct?"

"Gazala…"

"About Janus, your best friend, the professional knife thrower…"

"The Man With Two Faces."

"Do you know what's become of him?"

"He's dead."

"Really?"

"An unfortunate mishap in New York."

"Did his knife slip?"

I chuckled. "You've always had a sense of humor, Gazala. Actually, it was a poisoned dart. Blowguns do that."

She dragged on her cigarette, eyes narrowing.

"Are you certain he's dead, Tokol?"

"Of course. I saw the dart between his eyes myself."

"As usual, you're always so certain."

"A trait of us Midwesterners."

When the waiter came I ordered Château Latour Pauillac de Latour 1928, and, fortuitously, there was one bottle remaining, which I tasted and approved.

"Good old Tokol," Gazala said, "so predictable in your tastes, so American."

"My Kansan sensibilities."

We touched glasses.

"*Tchin*," she said.

Awkwardly, hesitantly, I said, "You mentioned something about, uh, a child?"

"Your conscience is clear, Tokol."

I saw the stone, hardly discreet, gleaming on her third finger.

"You're married now," I said.

"To a powerful man with many business interests."

"You also said you're still living on Rue de l'Abreuvoir."

"I did not give up my own *appartement* simply because of a matrimonial bond. There are times when I wish to be unattended or occupied otherwise."

"Now you're the one who's being secretive."

The fine wine, the shady warmth, and the prepossessing woman before me began to stir the old longing I had for her, which I had been certain was dormant. She reached across the table and took my hand.

"Tokol, I must tell you something."

"Yes, I feel the same—"

"No, no, no. Do not be stupid. I had planned to tell you nothing, to send you on your way in ignorance—but now, now I can't."

She squeezed my hand harder.

"They're going to kill you," she said.

"Is that all?" I chuckled. "It's already been tried. Many times."

"But before they do they want to know things about you."

"Such as?"

"Who you work for. Where your superiors can be found. What you know. You can gather the rest."

She released my hand.

"I betrayed you, Tokol."

"As if I hadn't reached that conclusion. And yet, yet I never would have suspected you, Gazala."

"When I saw you in the Abd al-Qadir Room of Le Saint George, I was angry, as much by your lies in the present as in the past. But now that I've been with you again…"

"Some small twinge of regret?"

"Tokol, I married a man with deeply adopted German attitudes. It was clear to me when I saw you again that you were in Algiers to work against the interests of my husband. He now refers to Germany as his Fatherland, something to him his own birthplace never was."

"Obviously, our meeting here was nothing but a setup."

She sighed. "But there is still time."

"For what?"

"For you to escape."

"You don't believe I'm worried about the gendarmes, do you? They're Keystone Kops."

"Not the police, Tokol. The Gestapo."

"In Algiers? Gestapo?"

"To fight the Jewish underground. You must go now, but not to the street from here in the garden. They're waiting for you just outside the gate. They intend to seize you the moment you leave. Enter the hotel from the garden and exit through the back door of the kitchen. The Gestapo has just one man inside."

"In a way, Gazala, I suppose I should thank you."

"If they catch you, you will not."

I was torn between kissing her and tearing out her heart.

"Go, Tokol."

"In a moment. Let me finish my Château Latour. It's awful damned expensive, you know."

"Something tells me you can afford it."

"Yeah, the diamond business paid off."

I quietly put *beaucoup* francs on the table.

Summoning the waiter, I asked for directions to the men's room. He pointed crudely, as waiters invariably do, and I excused myself and walked leisurely to the door leading inside the hotel, intending to give the impression I was merely headed to the *toilettes pour hommes.*

Inside, I detoured into the kitchen, where a door led to the rear of the hotel. The chef de cuisine, sous chef, line cook, prep cook, pastry chef, and their subalterns were busy at their fires when I burst in.

Suddenly, I heard a voice shout, "Halt or I will shoot. Hands in the air."

I turned.

A man in a dark overcoat and homburg was pointing a Luger straight at my heart. Several thoughts ran through my brain concurrently, foremost of which was that the Luger was the ugliest firearm ever made. He advanced, on his face a smile that was more of a scowl, and it was obvious he'd rather pump lead into my body than otherwise. But I knew his orders were to take me alive.

Snarling, he said, "You thought you could escape, eh, Herr Swan. Or should I call you Herr Tokoloshe? In addition, we have evidence that you are also Salaah al-Abdoo, the man who staged a brutal attack with a sword on a Waffen-SS enlisted man, carving into his buttocks a defilement of our hallowed symbol."

"Golly, where'd y'all hear that?"

"From a certain shopkeeper whom you visited regularly to drink his coffee. Disliking troublemakers who bring the authorities to the Casbah, he led us to the hovel you were sleeping in, and where we discovered a rare nimcha stolen from the Musée National des Antiquités. The reward for your arrest encouraged the coffee purveyor as well."

I shrugged my shoulders in my best aw-shucks manner.

"Frankly, Fritz, his coffee wasn't all that good. I prefer coffee thin enough to actually stir."

"Hans. My name is Hans."

"Say, I knew a guy named Fritz in New York. He's now at an exclusive resort called Dannemora. Anyway, Fritz, I don't think you have the guts to pull that trigger."

"I am inclined to do away with you here and now, you American pig. In fact... On your knees."

"Naw, Fritz, I'm not the type who kneels in prayer, but it won't bother me if you do. I'm gonna scram through that back door, so if you ice me you'll miss out on the latest Yankees scores."

"Scores?"

"Yeah, I get 'em by shortwave."

Pretty gutsy of me, I thought, as I turned my back, counting on the expectation that I was more valuable to the Gestapo alive than dead. Although to be truthful, I'd been wrong about such things before.

I heard a click, the gun cocking, and then a clunk and a thud.

The sous chef had clobbered Fritz on the skull with a cast-iron skillet.

"*Merci beaucoup*," I said.

"*Mes compliments, monsieur.*"

Not all French Algerians were fanciers of Nazis or Pétain.

Lacking time for further pleasantries, I dashed from the hotel and crossed the street into Le Jardin d'Essai du Hamma, pursued by the four agents positioned near the garden on the opposite side of the hotel.

I stopped under a date palm to retrieve the Smith and Wesson .38 special from my ankle holster.

Deciding to hold firm rather than running and risking a bullet in the back, I took a prone position, waited until I had a good shot, and dropped the first goon who came within firing range. That momentarily stopped them, but the three survivors began throwing iron wildly. Outnumbered, I was deluged by bullets whizzing above and around me. As the lead flew my ammo got low, and I realized I had become a sure bet for the Algerian carcass cart. Clearly, I wouldn't be able to hold them off much longer. So much confetti filled the air, I saw myself ever closer to the grisly task of worm counting.

Then I heard the rattle of a machine gun sounding a lot like a U.S. Ordnance M60. How did the cavalry happen to arrive just in time?

"Over here, Tokol. Quick!"

Calling to me was a man dressed identically to my dark-suited pursuers, and also wearing a homberg, shouldering an M60. My benefactor, apparently one of Henry Hyde's operatives, had arrived at the right moment. Hyde must have had him follow me to watch my back. Bless 'em both.

Lugers were no match for the M60, which could bring down a water buffalo herd, so in little time the bodies of all four Gestapo agents, oozing rivers of blood, lay sprawled on the ground.

Cautiously, I got up, holstered my Smith and Wesson, and went to my rescuer, who was loading fresh ammo links into the machine gun's feed tray, his back turned.

"Hey, fella," I said, "Don't know who you are, but you saved my ass."

"Don't you remember me, Tokol?" he said, turning.

It was Janus.

The

Man

With

Two

Faces

One of his faces grinned, the other did not.

Now his M60 was pointed directly at my midsection. Overkill, if you asked my opinion. Damned gun could tear apart a brick shithouse, and shitting bricks was something I was about to do.

"But, but you're dead," I said stupidly.

My stumbling assertion was imbecilic because he obviously wasn't, but in 1934 I had seen his staring-eyed corpse with its centrally-located dart following the Carnera-Baer bout in Long Island City, Queens. And here he was, six years after that fact, in Algiers and looking much the same. Only the dart was gone.

"Reports of my termination were immensely exaggerated, Tokol."

"You were buried in some empty lot by the East River."

"Obviously, I wasn't at my peak at that moment. But it's said all good things come to he who waits. And I've waited a long time for this."

"You're going to kill me."

"Of course. But not here. There's been enough bloodshed in this sublime park, and the *gendarmerie* will arrive momentarily. We're going elsewhere, you and I. There's much to catch up on."

"How are you going to get away with this? Marching me through the crowded streets of Algiers at the point of a hulking machine gun? That's nutty."

"Turn around. Now. Or I will kill you where you stand, much as it would break my heart."

He lied. When it came to me the man had no heart.

After I turned, I felt a blow to the back of my head, Janus taking me down in the way of George Raft reducing a heavy in a Warner Brothers gangster flick. Everything went black. That's all I knew until, with a throbbing headache, I came to. I was chained naked to some sort of chair, cold and metallic, and saw Janus standing over me while sipping wine in a long-stemmed crystal.

"It's a Domaine de la Romanee-Conti Montrachet, Tokol, Nineteen-Twenty-Four. I'm afraid I've drunk the bulk of the bottle, so a pity we can't share. And we once shared a lot, our booze, our women, our two bodies. Anyway, it was about time you woke up, not that I was worried, merely a bit impatient."

We were in a large room, blighted by the rubble of mosaics and stained glass, broken windows, crumbling walls, the roof intact but sagging.

"Where am I?"

"The ruins of the Tarik Ibn Zeyad Mosque in Hussein Dey, just east of Algiers. Tarik Ibn Zeyad, you may recall, was the Muslim military commander who invaded Gibraltar, then went on to conquer Cordoba, Granada, and Toledo. Alas, this mosque, which was named in his honor, fell into disuse, so I purchased it for my own machinations."

"What kind of chair do you have me in? Hurts all over like hell, and so do the chains on my wrists and ankles."

"I call it the Janus chair, my version of the Judas chair, occasionally known as the iron chair. The reason it hurts is that it's layered with thousands of sharpened needles on every side. By imperceptibly turning a winch, the needles slowly protrude, piercing the flesh of its, ah, seated victims. But worry not. There's a trough underneath to collect the blood."

"So you've given up throwing knives, Janus. Now you just turn a winch and let needles do your dirty work."

"Alas, my throwing arm has been irretrievably damaged. Due to you."

"All I know about your arm is that it enabled your hand to throw knives at me."

"Shall I tell you why I'm still alive instead, as you assumed, of being far below shoveling coal into the furnaces of Satan?"

"I'm dying to know."

"Odd choice of words, old boy, but you were always prescient. As you know, I was pierced by a dart launched by your associate, Miss Dryad, who has the reputation of performing with her lips omnipotent acts using a blowgun. It didn't quite kill me, but left me in a hypometabolic state in which the decay of my body, which gave every appearance of death, was temporarily arrested. The more reasoned among us compare it to hypothermia. Others call it suspended animation. Apparently, the poison on the dart's tip had that effect on me, something in my metabolism, singularly extraordinary. My rather coarse associates at the Garden Bowl were less lucky, all having been riddled with bullets unleashed by your friends.

"I gave every appearance of being dead, no pulse, no heartbeat, nary a breath. You can imagine my chagrin when I woke up amid a pile of corpses in a dark, shallow, poorly dug grave in a garbage-strewn Queens lot, as if no one cared whether our bodies were found. Somehow, I saw sky through a sliver of an opening in the dirt and rubble, suggesting I was not far from the surface. My throwing arm was contorted under a particularly heavy body, yet with my left hand I was able to claw my way out. My right arm never regained its strength, although my health improved as the effects of the poison wore off. But I was now alone and penniless in New York, my covetous associates quick to cash in on my presumed death, foreclosing on my assets, and abandoning me to the jackals.

"I imagine you were elated, thinking you were rid of me at last, yet I had a few tricks up the sleeve of my good arm, cashing in a number of IOUs, finally escaping aboard a tramp steamer to more hospitable environs in North Africa, our old stomping grounds. I experienced a long recuperation before beginning anew. But not for one second did I forget about you, not only how you destroyed my jungle princess, the love of my life—"

"Our lives."

"But left me to decompose in a mound of bloody corpses."

"You tried to kill me first, more than once."

"I intended to return for you someday, Tokol, encountering you when you least expected me. Then, lo and behold, you miraculously arrived in Algiers and fell into my lap like manna from Elysium. You have so much to pay for." He paused. "Oh, please excuse me while I adjust your chair's needles just a wee."

Instantly, I felt a thousand unrelenting pricks in my back, sides, and butt, although whether enough to draw blood I couldn't tell.

"Tokol, remind me to keep tightening the winch." He shook his head in annoyance, not at me but himself. "Chatting with you is so enjoyable, I tend to forget my obligations."

He sipped the wine, emptying the glass.

I said, "You got a fresh start here in Africa, Janus, and I'd almost congratulate you—if you weren't so despicable."

"I had many hidden resources here, which allowed me to achieve respectability and to marry well, all while investing in Germany, where the Third Reich has made it attractive for men of my ilk to make a fortune. I opened a headquarters in Frankfort, and commute regularly from there to here. No one is closer to Walther Funk, the Reich Minister of Economics, than I. And I now consider Germany to be my Fatherland— more than the America I came to despise."

"And yet in the park I saw you blow away those Gestapo thugs. Why save *my* life? Me, of all people?"

He minutely turned the winch again, and this time I felt even more tangible puncture wounds. I gritted my teeth.

"A pity about those Gestapo fellows, old boy, I being an auxiliary member and all, but I wanted you all to myself with no interference."

"You? Involved with the Gestapo? Makes no sense."

"The Jewish thing, naturally."

"You never had a bone to pick with the Jews. It was those crazy Southern evangelicals you despised. We both did. I mean, who in his right mind wouldn't?"

"When in Rome, Tokol... Now I'm a bonafide Nazi, founder of the Hitler Senior Citizens Association, President of the Third Reich Chess Club, and an active member of the Algiers branch of the Richard Wagner Society. Although, as you saw in the park, if anyone, Nazi or not, gets in my way... Rat, tat, tat. Overall, I find it advantageous to be on the winning side—and the domination of Europe is only the beginning of the Nazi's world empire."

"You always were a prick, Janus. I suspected it even when we were pals. You never told me you played chess."

"Ah, how young, brash, and impressionable we were. We had some high old times, didn't we, old boy? I'll always remember that night in Macau in the Pearl River Delta Hotel and Grill, just you, me, the Mandarin Boys Choir, the entire Macau Bats Rugby Team, and half of the Portuguese colonial military garrison. Everyone of us unclothed. A pity most of the photos didn't come out." Again he paused. "Excuse me, Tokol."

The screws tightened, the pins dug deeper, and now I felt streamlets of blood trickling down my flesh.

"This is really beginning to smart, you bastard. I'm starting to lose blood."

"Then all is well, which is the idea. Have you ever seen a body drained of blood? In life, through the skin, the veins appear as blue, but once the blood empties, turning red, the flesh becomes white, waxen, shrunken. That's what's happening to you even as we chat."

"I always knew *you* were bloodless, Janus, but at least I speak figuratively."

"I had intended to interrogate you on behalf of my friends in the Gestapo, imposing the most intense agony required to force you to spill your guts. But now I'm indifferent to what, if anything, you might reveal. My singular goal is to make you suffer dearly, in the process draining your corpse, a secondary pleasure.

"I'd thank you if it wasn't for the honor."

"Still cracking jokes, eh, Tokol. But before I crank the winch again, I'd like to introduce you to someone."

With his two faces, he simultaneously smiled and glowered in that familiar way I always knew.

"This isn't the time, Janus. I'm not dressed for visitors."

"Oh, you'll want to make an exception in this case."

"Are you talking about *Diana*? If you've done anything—"

"I'm speaking of my lovely wife. My dear," he called, "will you please honor us?"

From a screened off-area that I took to be the mosque's mihrab, in stepped...

Gazala.

I can't say I was surprised, although when she had mentioned her husband at the Hayreddin Barbarossa Hotel I never quite imagined he would be The Man With Two Faces—but everything was now clear to me.

She said, "Dear husband, is this really necessary? Couldn't you have let the Gestapo handle it? I thought that was our arrangement."

"The Gestapo was intruding. You know how they are. So pushy, crude, and ultimately stupid. I wanted Tokol in *this* place, on my own terms, and subject to my own methods."

"Your methods are cruel. I've watched you torture men in that awful chair creation of yours again and again. Often for sport. How many times have you made me empty the pan containing their blood?"

"Not *entirely* for sport, my dear. I needed to experiment to determine that the chair worked as I planned. It does. As for cruelty, it's something Tokol imposed on me, and now I'm repaying him."

He again tightened the winch, which resulted in such immense pain that I, normally stoic, except in bed, screamed. In time the needles would strike my vital arteries.

"Let him go, my dearest. Each of you has misused the other, and now both of you have too much pent up anger. I remember how close you were, how we all were. It is time to call it quits, agree that your lives turned in different directions, that you both behaved badly, and go your separate ways."

"Gazala, my dear, it's too late for all that. I'm enjoying myself too much. You know, I'm tempted to uncork another bottle of Domaine de la Romanee-Conti Montrachet. Ah, Tokol, I observe that you're bleeding freely now." He chuckled. "Your entire body is turning into a sieve."

Gazala said, "Janus, you must stop."

His shoulders stiffening, The Man With Two Faces said, "I am your husband, my dear. You may not tell me what to do. It is not your place. Particularly in Algeria."

"You think not?"

From behind her back she pulled a dainty jewel-encrusted, silver-plated revolver and pointed it at Janus's head.

He said, "Ah, you're holding that adorable ladies model Charter .32 Magnum caliber revolver I gave you for your birthday. It's about time you got some use out of it." He crossed his arms, a gesture that emanated a certain masculine intimidation. "Do you realize what you're doing by aiming it at me?"

"Fully."

"You leave me little choice, my dear. I shall have to punish you."

"You've punished me enough, Janus. I never wanted to learn chess. You've even threatened me with your torture chair."

"More than a threat, I'm afraid. Don't be surprised to find yourself sitting in it like our friend Tokoloshe here."

"You whipped me the other night for returning late from Mahjong."

"Of course. I shall not permit your disobedience. Or tardiness."

"You deprived me of my dinner and sent me to my room."

"Insubordination is not to be tolerated."

"Then, dear husband, now you will never again concern yourself with insubordination from anyone."

She fired a bullet into his brain.

Janus did not die an instant death. Before succumbing he said, "It's clear to me now. It was Tokol you always loved."

As he fell to the floor, the eyes of both of his faces flashed red on and off like those of a railroad's crossing signals before going black. Janus had underestimated her resolve even as he overestimated her love.

I was reasonably certain that this time he would not persevere in a state of suspended animation.

Gazala unchained me from the Janus chair, helped to staunch the bleeding from the uncountable number of pinholes in my flesh—it took a lot of styptic pencils—and got me dressed.

"You'll live, Tokol. Now leave. And get a tetanus shot. Maybe two."

"I must help you dispose of—"

"I will handle it. Go. And never return to Algiers."

When I last saw her, she was pouring my blood from the trough into a hole in the floor.

I felt a little weak, but having donated blood to the Red Cross, I knew it would pass.

My flight in the Navy Boeing 314 Clipper to London the following morning was uneventful, no ack-ack, no deviations, and despite the daily bombardments of the city by the Luftwaffe we landed safely on the Thames.

Diana and I had an exuberant reunion in her suite at Claridge's Hotel in Mayfair. She was in London to help the British war effort, in part schlepping kids from the city to the countryside to spare them from the Blitz.

"How's Kyle?" I asked.

"When I left, he was happily swallowing a gerbil. Poor baby must be lonely without me. Even king cobras need companionship. Tokee, darling, look what I brought you from the States."

Theatrically, she whipped the wraps from an advance experimental model Zenith Trans-Oceanic shortwave radio, with an auxiliary transmitter and microphone.

"Now you'll be able to get the scores from home," she said, "and talk to your cronies in Algiers."

Which would prove to be prophetic.

We disrobed, and as we collapsed on the sheets she ran her hand over my flesh.

"My god, Tokee, your body feels like an empty pincushion. There are tiny scabs everywhere. What happened to you?"

"Trust me, dollface, you don't want to know. The important thing is that I'm back with you."

Discreet, as always, Diana asked no more questions.

Pincushion aside, our lovemaking left us famished. Wartime conditions severely limited our customary dining habits, and the food in London was rationed, except bread and vegetables, with restaurant meals capped at five shillings. However, the COI saw that we received the requisite ration books, and Claridge's dining room did its best, often supplementing its pedestrian fare with caviar, lobsters, and oysters, which went unregulated.

More important, there was no ceiling on the consumption of gin, many bottles of which we drained in the company of Diana's Columbia network friend, Edward R. Murrow, who was never fazed no matter how many liters of spiritus frumenti went down his hallowed throat.

Aside from a few broken windows in our suite, like the

stiff-lipped Brits we coped with the Blitz. When we heard the air raid sirens we often decamped for Claridge's basement with the other hotel guests, including Holland's Queen Wilhelmina and Prince Bernhard, and the kings of Norway, Greece, and Yugoslavia. Sometimes, however, we preferred to watch the deadly fireworks from the roof.

One night, I tuned in the Zenith to reach Henry Hyde.

He hemmed and hawed, but finally revealed that the gendarmes had fished the body of a woman from the Bay of Algiers.

"The victim has been identified as the wife of a missing German industrialist who had residences in Frankfort and Algiers," he said. "She'd been shot in the back of the head. There have been no arrests. Sorry, Tokol. I think you knew her as Gazala Lazaar."

My heart sank. But only for a moment. I had a knack for recalibrating wretched news. Clearly, by giving me a warning about the Gestapo, Gazala had risked her life. But by killing her husband, The Man With Two Faces, she sealed her doom. I didn't share this unfortunate news with Diana, not that she wouldn't understand. But Gazala was part of my past, and better to leave it that way.

When we weren't actually observing the war from Claridge's rooftop, Diana and I got the latest via the Zenith, and not many of the headlines were good.

On clear, Sunday nights, when blessed by the gods of the ionosphere, we tuned in the shortwave transmission of the Blue Network in New York to listen to the familiar voice of…

Good evening, Mr. and Mrs. America and all the ships at sea. Let's go to press.

Flash! The Japanese Imperial Army has invaded French Indochina, currently governed by the Vichy. In China, the Nip-

ponese overran Shanghai and Nanking, and have set up a puppet state in Manchuria. It's going to take more than American Lend-Lease to bail out the Chinese. Now that Tokyo has signed the Tripartite Pact with Germany and Italy, how long will it be before the Japs move into Burma and the Philippines? Some observers believe Japan has Hawaii in its sights, but this observer says nuts to that. The Nips wouldn't have the guts.

Flash! Speaking of guts, this reporter's Certain Acquaintance has gone missing. I've learned that C.A., who was on a secret mission overseas, reportedly in Algiers, was planning to turn his attention to the Japs, perhaps even going to Tokyo itself to cause mischief. When he reappears you will hear it here first. Meanwhile, dear friend, may those who cursed you be cursed, and those who blessed you be blessed.

…For Jergens Lotion, this is Walter Winchell wishing you lotions of love.

FEDERAL BUREAU OF INVESTIGATION

MEMORANDUM

To: J. EDGAR HOOVER, Director
From: MIKE LITVAK, Special Agent
Date: October 31, 1942

Re: Tokoloshe and Son Cleansing Services

Regarding the disappearance of Mr. Tokol Tokoloshe
and his companion Miss Diana Dryad, there have been
new findings, although they do not adequately solve the
conundrum.

First, it is known by examining hotel records in London,
that Tokoloshe and Dryad late last year checked out of
Claridge's in Mayfair, and, apparently in disguise, left
England for North America on either an American troop
ship or a merchant vessel. Quite possibly on an aircraft
chartered by the COI, although its agents deny it.

Sometime in February of this year, Dryad terminated her
lease at Floyd Bennett Field in Marine Park, Brooklyn,
where she stored her plane, a Fairchild Model 45, and
flew it to parts unknown. At no time did Dryad file a flight
plan.

sIt should be noted that Dryad's pet king cobra Kyle is
currently lodged in the Central Park Zoo, and has struck
up a relationship with an emerald tree boa.

The pair turned up in Mexico City, where they stayed
in the Coyoacán district at La Casa Azul, the home of
artists Diego Rivera and Frida Kahlo, who reconciled
after their divorce. Their residence has long been under
surveillance. You may be interested to know that the
Russian exile Leon Trotsky lived in that house, where
he had an affair with Frida, prior to his assassination
in 1940. It is not known how long Tokol and Dryad
remained in Mexico before they flew to the Asian-Pacific
region.

While it is complicated, we have determined through
various airport records and intelligence reports that
Dyad's plane touched down in Cochin, China, as well
as Hong Kong, Singapore, Manila, Kuala Lumpur, and
Rangoon, but she always escaped to safety one step
ahead of the Japanese invaders. We can only speculate
that she and Tokoloshe journeyed from one crisis point to
another in order to independently assist in crippling the
Axis war machine.

But here is where it becomes murky.

The wreckage of Dryad's Fairchild was discovered by
a band of tribal natives led by a shaman on the small
Aleutian island of Oaxun, the nearest and most obscure
of the archipelago to Attu, which, as you know, was
seized by Japanese raiders on June 7 of this year, the

first time ever a foreign enemy has occupied American soil. According to the Aleuts, who consider Oaxun sacred land, the plane was badly damaged and appeared to have bullet holes in the fuselage. However, it is possible that Tokoloshe and Dryad survived the crash as no bodies were found. They may have been trying to reach Attu for the purpose of staging an act of sabotage against the Japanese garrison.

It is conceivable the two were taken into captivity by the Japanese troops bivouacked on Attu. This cannot be confirmed until American forces expel the Nipponese from the island, which may not ensue until sometime next year.

I am afraid, sir, I must end this report inconclusively, but our special task force will remain fully alert until the mystery of Tokol Tokoloshe and Diana Dryad is entirely resolved or you retire from the FBI, not that any of us wishes to see you go.

Respectfully,

M. Litvak

Mike Litvak, Special Agent

ACKNOWLEDGMENTS

With grateful recognition to my fellow scribes in the esteemed Bucks County Writers Workshop for their dedication to the written word while in pursuit of literary excellence. Especial thanks to Parisian-born Daniel Dorian for his knowledge of Algiers, and to my sibling, Steve, a connoisseur of pipeline valves.

AUTHOR

Don Swaim is the author of *The Assassination of Ambrose Bierce: A Love Story* (Hippocampus Press), *The H.L. Mencken Murder Case* (St. Martins Press), and other titles and tales. A Kansan by birth, Ohioan by education, Manhattanite by inclination, and Pennsylvanian by preference, Don is curator of the Internet's definitive *Ambrose Bierce Site*, founder of the venerable Bucks County Writers Workshop, and voice of CBS Radio's "Book Beat."